What the critics are saying...

5 Unicorns "Love and Rockets was so thoroughly satisfying, I can't say enough good things about it. Charlene Teglia has written a contemporary romance that delivers love, romance, sensuality and humor..." ~ *Melissa, Enchanted in Romance*

"LOVE AND ROCKETS was a genuinely enjoyable, heartwarming and unforgettable book. I will remember these remarkable characters for a long time to come. I can hardly wait for more from the WHEN SPARKS FLY series and from the very funny and very talented Charlene Teglia." ~ *Miaka, Romance Junkies*

4 Cups of Coffee "When Sparks Fly - Love and Rockets is different from many contemporaries ...It is just a great, sweet romance with strong writing and wonderful dialogue...This is a definite keeper." ~ *Anya Khan, Coffee Time Romance*

"The two meet at the company party and the exchange is hilarious...The jaded playboy is ready for real love and the ambitious and absentminded redhead is ready to experience love and life...The story is very sensual and also very touching. It's clear from the first encounter that these two people will entertain you until the end and of course you can expect fireworks in bed!" ~ *Sarah, Mon-Boudoir*

4.5 Unicorns "Love and Rockets is a fantastic story filled with humor and hot sex. The building relationship between Anna and Jay was in turns funny and intense. Charlene Teglia has brought into being a fantastic romance that grabbed me from the first and didn't release me in the end... I highly recommend this highly amusing and hot book!!" ~ *Lyonene, Enchanted in Romance*

4 Unicorns "...I love Jay's quirky sense of humor and the way he confuses Anna at every turn. Anna is too serious and needs to have her world shaken up in a big way. The only thing that could make this book any better is another book. Congratulations Charlene." ~ *Laura, Enchanted in Romance*

4 Angels "Love and Rockets is an exceptional beginning to Charlene Teglia's new series, *When Sparks Fly*. The deep emotional element of the story will have you hating to put this book down. ...I look forward to the next installment of this series." ~ *Tewanda, Fallen Angel Reviews*

Charlene Teglia

Love and Rockets

When Sparks Fly

ELLORA'S CAVE
ROMANTICA PUBLISHING

An Ellora's Cave Romantica Publication

www.ellorascave.com

When Sparks Fly: Love and Rockets

ISBN #1419952382
ALL RIGHTS RESERVED.
When Sparks Fly: Love and Rockets
Copyright© 2005 Charlene Teglia
Edited by: Sue-Ellen Gower
Cover art by: Syneca

Electronic book Publication: February, 2005
Trade paperback Publication: August, 2005

Excerpt from *Dangerous Games*
Copyright © Charlene Teglia, 2005

With the exception of quotes used in reviews, this book may not be reproduced or used in whole or in part by any means existing without written permission from the publisher, Ellora's Cave Publishing, Inc.® 1056 Home Avenue, Akron OH 44310-3502.

This book is a work of fiction and any resemblance to persons, living or dead, or places, events or locales is purely coincidental. The characters are productions of the authors' imagination and used fictitiously.

Warning:

The following material contains graphic sexual content meant for mature readers. *Love and Rockets* has been rated *S-ensuous* by a minimum of three independent reviewers.

Ellora's Cave Publishing offers three levels of Romantica™ reading entertainment: S (S-ensuous), E (E-rotic), and X (X-treme).

S-*ensuous* love scenes are explicit and leave nothing to the imagination.

E-*rotic* love scenes are explicit, leave nothing to the imagination, and are high in volume per the overall word count. In addition, some E-rated titles might contain fantasy material that some readers find objectionable, such as bondage, submission, same sex encounters, forced seductions, etc. E-rated titles are the most graphic titles we carry; it is common, for instance, for an author to use words such as "fucking", "cock", "pussy", etc., within their work of literature.

X-*treme* titles differ from E-rated titles only in plot premise and storyline execution. Unlike E-rated titles, stories designated with the letter X tend to contain controversial subject matter not for the faint of heart.

Also by Charlene Teglia:

Dangerous Games

About the author:

Charlene Teglia writes erotic romance with humor and speculative fiction elements. She can't imagine any better life than making up stories about hunky Alpha heroes who meet their match and live happily ever after, whether it happens right next door, in outer space, or the outer limits of imagination. When she's not writing, she can be found hiking around the Olympic Peninsula with her family or opening and closing doors for cats.

Charlene welcomes mail from readers. You can write to her c/o Ellora's Cave Publishing at 1056 Home Avenue, Arkon OH 44310-3502.

Love and Rockets
When Sparks Fly

Trademarks Acknowledgement

The author acknowledges the trademarked status and trademark owners of the following wordmarks mentioned in this work of fiction:

Bugs Bunny: Time Warner Entertainment Company

Disney World: Walt Disney Productions

Elmer Fudd: Time Warner Entertainment Company

GQ: Advance Magazine Publishers Inc.

James Bond: DANJAQ S.A.

Kodak: Eastman Kodak Company

L.L. Bean: L.L. Bean, Inc.

MENSA: American MENSA Limited

Miata: Mazda Motor Corporation

Nikes: Nike, Inc

Victoria's Secret: V Secret Catalogue, Inc.

Chapter One

Anna Leslie was having a really bad day.

In fact, she mused, she might be setting some kind of record.

First of all, it was mud season. In other parts of the country, they had spring. In the extreme northeastern part of America, however, it just went from snow tire season to mud season. Right before black fly season. Which said it all.

Anna wished with all her heart just then that she'd never left California, where the only problems were droughts and earthquakes. Earthquakes weren't so bad. A little tremor now and then kept a person on their toes. And kept shelves from collecting too much clutter. True, there was the occasional difficulty on the LA freeway and the fruit police on the border who'd confiscate a wayfaring banana from the unwary traveler.

But all in all, it didn't seem bad in comparison to mud season.

Gazing mournfully at the mud encasing her formerly white running shoes, she reflected that she should have seen it coming.

It was Monday, after all.

Not that she'd known it was Monday right away. She tended to forget to remove the previous day's sheet from her daily calendar. Her lab assistant, Jane, usually did that. Anna let them pile up until Jane finally came and frenziedly tore sheet after sheet off until she found the actual, current date.

Anna had tried to explain that she wasn't terribly interested in time since it wasn't her field. She left it to the theorists. But Jane just shook her head and told her boss that she had to get out more.

Well, she'd gotten out today and the world was full of melting slush and mud. She really didn't see much point in going back out there on purpose any time soon.

Now it seemed she didn't have a choice.

Glumly, Anna looked again at the invitation that had been waiting for her when she arrived at work, evidently for the sole cosmic purpose of topping the traffic, the mud, her ruined Nikes and the bad karma of Mondays in general.

It was pretty, she had to admit that. The midnight blue background showed off the neon streaks of color that depicted a fireworks display lighting up the night. Glittering gold cursive lettering read, "You're Invited!"

She flipped it open, already knowing what she'd find inside. She read it anyway with a growing sense of doom.

"Frontier Fireworks celebrates its twentieth birthday."

She stopped and sighed. She really wasn't up to this.

"From seven to midnight, an open bar and buffet in the penthouse for all department heads and company officers is our way of saying Thank You for another successful year."

There was a note on the invitation indicating that she could bring a date.

Maybe, Anna thought hopefully, she could just *send* a date.

A handwritten note at the bottom demanded her continued attention. She read on, "Anna, don't give me any excuses this year. I don't care if you have a note from your doctor, you will be present for this company function or I'll cut your funding. Go buy a new dress and save me a dance."

The lecturing note didn't have a signature.

It didn't need one.

It was from Lyle Grant, the scold-happy founder and president of Frontier Fireworks.

Anna thought wistfully that making an appointment with her dentist wouldn't work this year. If Lyle said he'd cut her funding, he meant it. He might be gruff and blustery, not to mention occasionally heavy-handed in his choice of words, but he didn't make idle threats.

He probably also knew it was the only way to get her out of her lab.

Well, it was easy for him to order her to go shopping, buy a slinky evening gown and dance the night away. He didn't know what it was like.

Anna wished again that she hadn't left California. She'd blended in there. It was the plastic surgery capital of the world.

Here in Maine, a six-foot redhead with a body like Venus and a face that cried "cover girl" stuck out like an Amazon. In the world of business, it was even worse.

She didn't look like the scientist in charge of Research and Development at Frontier Fireworks.

She looked like a high-priced call girl.

Anna looked at the invitation again and wanted to cry.

It wouldn't be so bad if she could hide in one of her shapeless lab coats but it was strictly black tie and she had what she knew perfectly well was a direct order to attend in formal evening dress.

She silently cursed Lyle and his whole company. She'd be tempted to let his threat backfire on him and leave but she was working on something really special. A longer-lasting, more vibrant blue as the final color in a combination red, white and blue rocket. She planned to call it the Freedom Finale.

It was a real pyrotechnic challenge.

Anna couldn't walk away from a challenge.

Her work was a dream come true. She created the colorful and noisy rockets used in big fireworks displays. The job combined chemistry, physics and thermodynamics and it was as much an art form as applied science. It was an ancient art that went back as far as the Sung dynasty and Anna deeply, passionately and wholeheartedly loved her work.

Lyle couldn't have threatened her with anything worse and he knew it, the fiend.

Jane reappeared with two cups of herbal tea, took one look at her long face and let out a whistle. "Hey, who died?"

Anna wordlessly waved the invitation at Jane and took her cup of tea.

"Oh, the annual bash! Great, you'll have a ball. And look, you get to take the afternoon off to go shopping. Anna, that's wonderful!" Jane enthused.

"Wonderful. Just the word I was thinking of," she grumbled in reply.

Jane gave her an impatient look. "Come on, you live like a hermit and you practically have to be forced out of here at gunpoint. You work too hard. You should get out more, enjoy your success."

"Jane, it was awful that last time I went. That's why I used the dentist excuse last year. The other VIPs are all men and they were either patting me on the head or pinching my rear."

"So take a big, strong date to protect you and defend your honor."

Maybe that wasn't a bad idea. "Do you have anybody in mind?" Anna asked curiously.

"You could take my twin," Jane suggested.

"Isn't he dating somebody?"

"John would break a date with Sandra Bullock for you. He likes you. He gets to be the protective big brother with you that he never got a chance to with me." Jane leaned forward and stage-whispered, "I know you probably haven't noticed but I'm kind of pushy and assertive and I always fought my own battles before he could."

That got a smile from Anna. Although she looked like an Amazon, in truth she wasn't much on confrontation. She wished she was more like Jane. The plucky brunette would take whatever any man who tried to patronize her dished out and serve it right back in his face.

Her vivacious assistant was everything she wasn't. She was six inches shorter, to begin with. A cap of curly dark hair set off an oval face and sparkling blue eyes that could light with the fire of battle in an instant. Jane had the temperament of a little terrier that doesn't know it can't take on a Doberman.

"What I need isn't a date," Anna mused. "I need a course in assertiveness training."

She was half-joking as she said it but it dawned on her that from the depths of her subconscious mind she'd spoken the truth.

She was a big girl, in more ways than one. She should be fighting her own battles. Why should she let anyone intimidate her or talk down to her? Jane was right. She'd worked long and hard for her success and she deserved to enjoy it.

What did those men have that she didn't have, besides the obvious physical differences? None of them could replace her in a job that blended three scientific disciplines with the added element of artistic mastery.

She was hardworking, productive, creative and brilliant.

She was a valuable asset to the company.

She was woman. Maybe it was time they heard her roar.

Anna took another sip of her tea.

"Jane," she said, "I need the local directory and the phone. I'm taking the afternoon off. I'm going shopping."

"Fantastic!"

"And I'm going to see a therapist."

Jane stopped dead in her tracks. "You're kidding. This is a joke, right?"

"No, it's not a joke. I'm going to make an appointment and go see a therapist. Immediately. I'm a crisis case."

"Anna, you're talking about seeing a shrink," Jane pointed out, as if she might have missed that obvious detail.

"Everybody does it in California," Anna answered stubbornly. "Even busboys have therapists there."

"May I point out this is Maine? We do things a little different around heah." Jane deliberately used the local pronunciation to emphasize her point.

"Well, I'm not from around 'heah'." Anna stated the obvious with a determined air. "And I'm not afraid to admit it if I need help. I need help, Jane. This is ridiculous. I'm six-foot tall and twenty-eight years old. I'm an adult and I need to learn to stand up for myself."

In fact, now that she thought about it, it occurred to her that she needed all kinds of professional help.

"Jane, what's the name of that big beauty salon? I need a facial, a manicure, a makeover and I need to get my hair done." Her waist-length flaming mane lay in a long, ropy braid at the moment. Practical for lab work, but hardly the thing for a party dress.

She considered other possibilities. Maybe a pedicure, too. A loofah treatment. A massage.

She was starting to warm to the idea of going all out and letting her hair down. Why not? She was entitled. In fact, she'd like to see anybody try to stop her. Determination took root and grew until it solidified in immovable decision.

Once she made up her mind about something, she stuck to it. Her redheaded stubbornness, no doubt. The more Anna thought about it, the more ridiculous she felt for letting a handful of Neanderthal leftovers intimidate her. What was she, a woman or a mouse?

Woman, Anna decided firmly.

She would not hide in a shapeless lab coat for the rest of her days. She had a body to be proud of. So it wasn't model skinny. It was better. Not even remotely straight-lined in quasi-masculine, androgynous style. It was boldly full-blown and shaped in dangerous curves that declared femininity in no uncertain terms.

And what was wrong with that?

Suddenly, the frustration of years of dissatisfaction and discomfort with her own body and her own sexuality boiled up and overflowed.

She'd never been able to wear a suit and look masculine. So she'd be feminine to the hilt. She'd never been able to look most people in the eye without bending down. So she'd stand tall and even wear heels if she darn well felt like it. With her hair and her figure, not to mention her face, she'd never blend in with the background. The only solution was to make the most of it and learn to enjoy center stage.

By God, she'd upstage Lyle tonight and love it.

Jane returned with the phone and the directory. "You're really going to do it? Go in for the full beauty treatment?"

"I am. The works," Anna announced. "And then I'm going to buy the reddest, slinkiest dress I can find and the highest, skinniest heels."

The ultimate in forbidden for the toweringly tall and the blindingly redheaded.

Anna was on a roll now.

"I'm going to dance and drink champagne. I'm going to go alone and stand on my own two feet. And I'm signing up for self-defense training, too, so any man who tries to pinch my behind had better move fast or lose a hand."

Jane whistled and clapped. "Go get 'em! You're my hero. But you need to sign these first."

Jane snagged a pile of papers from her "in" tray and slid them in front of Anna, separating them to the proper page for each signature. Anna dutifully signed them without looking, her mind focused on party strategy.

It was too bad she hadn't decided to get into the spirit of the party sooner, Anna reflected. She'd known it was coming up for weeks. She could have set up a dramatic entrance with a flash and a puff of colored smoke. Nothing too big or flammable. Just the kind of thing used in stage magic.

Well, tonight she'd leave chemistry in her lab and go for a different kind of special effect.

And Lyle Grant would rue the day he'd used an underhanded ultimatum on her.

She'd dance his feet off.

Then she'd leave a little smoking surprise in his office. Something with a self-consuming remote switch she could trigger from afar. Just as a little reminder about who he was messing with.

With an evil chortle, the mad scientist sat down and started to make phone calls.

So he wanted her to go to his party? She'd show these Yankees how to party. In California, it was an avocation. No, a profession. A calling.

She didn't really regret the fact that she'd made the move to the east coast instead of doing Hollywood special effects or going to do pyrotechnics for NASA.

Something about Maine deeply appealed to Anna, in spite of the snow and mud. It had a sense of history, of roots. Portland was a fairly typical city but in most places in Maine, a person who'd been there ten years was still a newcomer and could expect to be referred to as "the one who bought the old Johnson place".

Perversely, Anna liked that. And the state had a rugged beauty, from the mountains to the rocky Atlantic coast. It had drama and it bred hardiness.

She sometimes felt as out of place as a hothouse flower dropped in the wilds but that was what her little rebellion was all about.

She was different. She couldn't change it but she could change how she felt about it. She'd be different all the way and like it. Celebrate her unique self.

And she'd go see a therapist about assertiveness and confrontation if she felt like it.

Right after she went to the salon for every service they offered.

It took quite a while to get the full treatment. Anna had plenty of time to think while she was wrapped in a mudpack as a preliminary to being loofahed within an inch of her life.

She felt like she'd shed old insecurities with every layer of skin.

She got a massage with an oil that, according to the believers in aromatherapy, would relax and revitalize her.

She had her long hair washed and styled in an intricate weave that made a net from the sides and ran down the center of her back.

A professional makeup artist gave her an updated look, since Anna hadn't bothered to change the colors or techniques she used since she started wearing makeup.

And she got a manicure, including a cuticle massage.

With every step, Anna felt transformed. She was being remade in a new image. An image of confidence. An image of being comfortably at home in her own skin.

She was a hardworking professional woman who made very good money. She should pamper herself more. Besides, Anna decided, it was about time that she started dressing for success. At least, as far as she could. Lab work demanded rather casual dress. But that didn't mean she had to let herself go completely.

And she could practice making a few demands for a change instead of quietly going about her business as usual. Where had that approach gotten her? Even the janitor had a better parking space than she did. She should ask for a new one, closer to her lab and free of mud, while she was at it. She hadn't asked for anything in the three years she'd been with Frontier.

In fact, Anna realized soberly, she hadn't been in the habit of asking for what she needed, wanted or deserved, ever.

Exactly the problem.

Well, she was going to start asking. She was going to learn how to communicate, negotiate and delegate.

While she was at it, maybe she'd take a short course in group dynamics, too. She needed every advantage to overcome the dual handicaps her looks and intellect presented. The unfortunate truth was that she made people uncomfortable. And in business, cooperation depended on a comfortable work relationship.

Since she was the person with the problem, Anna decided, it was clearly her responsibility to learn how to put people at ease and to relate better. She couldn't just go on not dealing with people because she didn't know how.

Besides, her life couldn't revolve around staying absorbed in work forever. She'd wind up a lifeless old biddy, hunched over her worktable. One who spent every evening, weekend and holiday alone and had no friends.

If it wasn't for Jane, that would be true now.

The outgoing brunette had taken her boss under her wing and dragged her out to movies on weekends. Her family insisted on including her for Thanksgiving and Christmas. Jane's fraternal twin, John, had taken on a big brother role in Anna's life and she knew if she'd asked him, he would have gone with her to the party and defended her from anyone who tried to pat her on either end.

But she couldn't lean on Jane and John forever. It wasn't fair. She knew she was capable of mastering communication skills. Compared to rocket science, how hard could it be?

When the salon had done all they could for her, Anna paid the bill without a single twinge and moved on to shopping.

Her first step had to be the dress, she decided. Then she'd get the accessories and lingerie to match.

It was easy to find the right dress, so much so that it amazed her. The very first formal shop that Anna went into, her eye went directly to the flame sheath.

Anna moved toward the dress like a woman in a trance.

It was absolutely perfect.

The satin gown had thin spaghetti straps of delicate ribbon and a wonderfully low bodice. Sequins spangled the body of the dress. And lastly, it sported fringed trim around the hem in true flapper style that ended mid-thigh. It could have come straight out of the roaring twenties.

She felt a thrill of acquisitiveness posses her.

It was the most beautiful evening dress she'd ever seen and she had to have it.

For once, Anna actively looked for a saleswoman. She easily found one, sporting the typical sales uniform of tailored navy specifically designed to make salespeople everywhere look like interchangeable cogs in the cosmic shopping machine.

As if dressing salespeople like clones encouraged shoppers to trust their advice on fashion.

Anna waved the woman over and indicated the dress. "I want to try this on."

When the saleswoman questioned her color choice and happened to mention her hair, Anna smiled dangerously. "Yes, I know it's red. I want red. I love red." She looked at the price tag and added, "Don't you get a commission on sales?"

Incredible. She was getting bolder by the minute. She was finally coming into her own and living up to her red-haired heritage. About time, too. She'd actually looked for a salesperson instead of avoiding one. She'd defended her choice in the face of disapproval, although it didn't take much to overlook the wardrobe wisdom of a navy-suited contestant for Miss Invisibility. To her vast surprise and growing delight, she, Anna Leslie, had actually used a little financial strong-arming.

Maybe there was hope for her.

When she tried the dress on and got a look at her reflection in the three-sided mirror, her resolve deepened. The fiery color was the perfect foil for her hair. Wasn't it her job to know colors? Out of all the subtle shades of red there were, some had to complement her hair. And this one did.

Anna saw a stranger looking back at her. Sophisticated, poised and elegant. Confident and assured.

She saw a woman who looked like she could do anything she set her mind to.

It was a pleasure to buy the gown. For a stronger sense of confidence, she would have paid twice as much. She'd gotten a steal.

From the formal wear shop, Anna headed to the lingerie shop and found a merry widow that matched the dress. She'd always worn traditional, plain underwear. But the new her, and the new dress, definitely called for bold lingerie.

Feeling bolder by the minute, Anna chose stockings a flapper would have worn, thigh-high with a back seam. Feminine garters completed the costume.

Now, she just had to find the perfect shoes.

Anna marched into the nearby shoe store, waved down another navy suit and loudly requested the highest heels they had in a size ten.

She was really getting good at this.

After trying on several pairs of shoes, Anna finally settled on impossibly soft Italian leather pumps in the same shade as the evening dress with fragile three-inch heels. She would have worn higher heels, but she wasn't used to them and they hurt her back with the enforced arch they produced.

She figured she'd work up to those with practice.

Anna towered over everyone in the shoe store when she tried them on and she loved it.

She looked down at the helpful navy-suited clerk and said, "I'll take these."

It was a lift in more ways than one.

How long had it been since she'd experienced the psychological boost getting a beauty treatment provided? When was the last time she'd felt the heady joy of shopping for a special occasion and finding the perfect outfit?

Far too long ago, evidently. As big a problem in its own way as not asking for what she wanted. Maybe her one-sided lifestyle had something to do with her lack of confidence. Her tunnel vision focus on work wasn't healthy. She loved her work. It was challenging, exciting and rewarding. But she had other needs, other sides to her personality that had obviously been neglected for far too long.

Well, it was never too late to start. From now on, she'd take better care of herself. Treat herself the way she deserved to be treated. All work and no play had made her a very dull girl. The time had come to play as hard as she'd been working.

It was never too late to start, was it?

Committed to the new Anna, whoever that might turn out to be, she practically skipped back to her sporty Miata, gloating over her purchases all the way.

Lyle was going to choke when he got a load of her dress.

Eldon in Accounting would probably faint.

Anna could hardly wait.

Meanwhile, she really did need some pointers on communication and assertiveness, and as a dedicated researcher the obvious answer was to go straight to an expert source. However, the source she'd consult would be the local bookstore.

She really didn't think she needed her head shrunk. She just needed some knowledge. Some expertise she could glean and put into practice.

She didn't think it should take her too long to learn what she needed to put into practice. She'd get some pointers and then set about mastering the techniques she needed to be more self-confident and assertive.

Judging from today's experiences, it was largely a matter of attitude, anyway.

The bookstore offered all sorts of choices. Anna read through several titles and found her eye drawn to one about becoming a bad girl.

Intrigued, she pulled it down and flipped through some of the pages.

Amazing. It seemed she wasn't the only one who'd suddenly gotten fed up with staying quietly in the background, nose to the grindstone. Someone else had felt strongly enough to write a book about it.

A smile tugged at the corner of her generous mouth. Well, why not? She was tired of doing the right thing and being good. But she'd been doing it for so long that she might actually need to consult a guide to badness.

Anna tucked the book under her arm and looked at a few others. A book on the differences between men and women. Amen to that, she thought silently. Different as in possibly genuinely alien species. But if she wanted to improve her communication skills, she should learn something about how the other species worked.

She felt certain that it wasn't all that different from physics. Behavior was governed by a set of clearly defined laws. Cause and effect, for example. Once she knew the laws involved, she'd understand the causes and be able to predict and even direct the effect.

Anna sorted through the rest of the selection and added a book on understanding body language to her stack.

Well, that ought to cover the basics, anyway, even for a total recluse.

Her shopping finished, Anna headed for home.

Maybe Lyle's arbitrary command had been just the challenge she needed to stir her to action. The invitation to the party was leading her to a whole new life. As such, it deserved to be celebrated with style.

On a sudden whim, Anna decided to rent a limo for the occasion. Too much champagne and she'd need the driver anyway. It was the finishing touch to the feeling of Cinderella going to the ball.

She thought of her fragile, beautiful new shoes and made a mental note to request a very large, strong driver. They were her glass slippers and she wasn't about to slog through the mud in them.

According to her watch, by the time she called for the limo and dressed she'd be just tardy enough to make a grand entrance.

A very gleeful Amazon gathered up her assorted packages and headed into her townhouse. The message light on her answering machine was flashing and she pushed the playback button as she passed.

Lyle's nail-spitting voice crackled out at her in full lecture mode.

"Dammit, Anna, what's this Jane tells me about you being at some appointment? I told you, I won't take that lame excuse this year. You be at that party or I'll drag you there myself, do you hear? I don't care if you have wisdom teeth, or an IRS audit, or purple spots from head to toe. You just show up. Why I have to make you get dressed up and have some fun, I don't know. So help me—"

Abruptly, the message reached its time limit and cut him off, which must have annoyed him considerably. He loved a captive audience and hated it when one managed to escape.

A ripple of laughter escaped her. Well, that was one way to get around Lyle's infamous lectures.

He'd be surprised when she turned up, all decked out.

Although knowing the man, he'd be certain that his thorough lecture was responsible for her appearance.

Moments later, the limousine rental dealt with, Anna was still laughing in delighted anticipation as she went off to complete her fairy-tale transformation. Then she'd await the arrival of her pumpkin coach. Although at the rate they were charging her, if it quit after midnight somebody was going to hear about it.

She had confrontation techniques to practice.

Chapter Two

When Anna walked through the door and made her entrance, it went better than anything in her wildest dreams.

Every eye turned and clung to the vision in a symphony of flame. A magic prop would have spoiled the effect, she decided. The dress was a showstopper.

And maybe a heartstopper. She hoped old Bill Whittaker had his bottle of nitroglycerine pills. He looked like palpitations were setting in again.

She lounged in the doorway as if she'd been doing this all her life and reveled in the deafening silence as conversation stopped, glasses and forks froze in midair and the band took ten.

Her cool violet gaze swept the room and settled on her prey.

There he was, the blustering bag of wind, gaping at her with one of his disgusting cigars smoldering, forgotten, in his hand.

Good. Maybe he'd set fire to his tuxedo. Then he'd be sorry he'd held her funding over her head.

In fact, Anna decided as she began a graceful, deliberate stalk reminiscent of a leopard closing in on a gazelle, he'd be sorry anyway. She was going to get a better parking spot, more titanium and she'd think of something else, too. Make him send her to Disney World to watch the fireworks and take notes, maybe.

She'd never been to Florida.

She sashayed dangerously over to a completely flabbergasted Lyle Grant and crooked a finger through his bowtie.

"I believe you wanted to dance."

Lyle just continued to stare at her with bulging eyes.

"I believe I'll call the tune." Her musical voice was deadly with double meaning.

Anna turned to engage the rapt attention of the band's leader.

"Fly Me to the Moon?"

The man swallowed and answered hoarsely, "I'll gift wrap it for you."

Then he got a hold of himself and the band swung into the classic tune.

Anna floated around the dance floor with her paralyzed victim following her lead.

She casually unwrapped the silk tie and toyed with the ends, using them to steer a dumbstruck Lyle.

"You threatened my funding." She regarded him steadily from the advantage of high ground and wondered why on earth she hadn't capitalized on her height before. The heels added to the edge.

Lyle didn't respond.

A silken flick on his cheek with the end of the tie punctuated her next statement. "That was naughty."

Lyle looked like he was on the verge of collapse.

He really didn't know how to take the sudden transformation, Anna realized.

Laughing inwardly, she continued in a thoughtful voice, "Now you're going to have to make it up to me."

She let him stew for a few minutes while she continued to waltz like Ginger in her finest hour.

"Larry the janitor has a better parking spot than I do, Lyle."

She paused and let that sink in.

"I want a new one. I ruined my Nikes today."

She tightened her hands in the narrow strip of silk until he was in danger of being garroted and murmured softly, "I love my Nikes, Lyle."

A strangled sound escaped him.

She smiled sweetly.

"I knew you'd understand."

Anna was getting into her bad girl role and having the time of her life. Why hadn't she ever done anything like this before? For once she had the roaring Lyle Grant speechless. Helpless. On the receiving end of her kind of lecture.

The sensation of power was a heady experience.

She decided to take pity on the man. He was all bluster and underneath he was no match for her.

Anna retied his silk bow carefully as they finished the dance, if it could be called dancing. "I'm thirsty. I need some champagne," she informed Lyle. In parting, she brushed a kiss on his leathery cheek before strolling away in search of whatever other thrills and opportunities the evening held.

Lyle remained rooted in place behind her. One hand slowly came up to touch the cheek her lips had grazed.

To the sardonic eye of one observer, it was a very touching scene.

"It looks like our fearless leader has annoyed that luscious armful," Jay remarked casually to the group of fellow workers he'd just been introduced to before the bombshell made her explosive entry. The new vice-president of marketing sympathized inwardly with the man's plight. He wouldn't want the bombshell annoyed with him.

He continued, "I predict he buys her a rock with more carats than Bugs Bunny eats in a year."

Instead of the expected laughter at his wisecrack, there was a derisive snigger or two and a choking, wheezing sound from the accounting manager at his right.

"That's—that's Miss Firecracker," the accounting manager, Eldon, finally managed to say. He looked at Jay as if he'd just insulted the Queen Mother.

"No kidding," Jay drawled, eyeing the Amazon with the appreciative eye of a connoisseur. "She does look like one hot little honey, all right."

More sniggers met that remark, and induced more choking from Eldon.

"Miss Firecracker, hmm? I don't have to ask how she came by that name. It looks like she's lighting up Grant's nights," Jay went on, encouraged. He could never pass up an opportunity to expose his wit.

"He's obviously carrying some torch," he continued. "I hope there's a fire extinguisher nearby."

He paused for the laughter to subside before he delivered his next line. "I don't have to ask what position she represents. From here I'd say it looks like Female

Superior. He's a brave man to let a woman like that be on top."

Eldon interrupted his amateur comedy hour by tugging on his tuxedo sleeve hard enough to threaten the fabric.

"Stop! She works for Frontier."

Jay laughed. "I bet she does! She looks like a woman who enjoys her work, too."

The innuendo had the sniggerers roaring. Eldon looked horrified.

"No, she does," he persisted. "She's—"

"A working girl," Jay interrupted. "Say no more, my good man, I completely understand. A stunning representative of an old and honorable profession."

His dark eyes examined the fiery piece of work speculatively as she tipped back her head and drained a crystal glass of its sparkling contents.

Maybe Grant's loss would be his gain.

"Since she seems a little put out with Grant, maybe she'd be open to another opportunity," Jay mused out loud.

Whatever the price, he was certain she'd be worth every penny. Miss Firecracker was incendiary with a capital I. Explosive. He could feel the heat from clear across the room.

The stunning siren seemed to feel his predatory gaze.

She turned and met his eyes coolly from her position by the bar. The eyes that boldly met and held his glowed like jewels.

Amethyst, Jay thought in distraction. Beautiful.

He admired her undulating curves as she approached and held out her hand to him. Jay took it and carried it to his lips, continuing to hold her unusual eyes as he did.

"We haven't been introduced."

She had a voice like warm honey. It was too much. Was there anything she didn't have? Jay's appreciation for her various attributes grew.

"Miss Firecracker, isn't it?" He stated her nickname boldly. "Jay Whitman at your service. Or maybe I could persuade you to be at my service, since things seem to have gone wrong with your patron, there."

Something indefinable glittered in the jeweled depths of her eyes.

"My patron?"

Heat spread through him at the thought of her fiery kisses burning his skin and her honeyed voice crying out in passion.

"Are you asking if I'm for sale?" Her smooth voice had gone even and tight with anger but Jay didn't notice.

Instead, he laughed.

His dark eyes gleamed with mingled desire and amusement as he informed her soberly, "Honey, there's no doubt about what you're here for. Just who."

"Really."

She gazed at him thoughtfully and Jay noticed she matched his considerable height easily in her heels.

She continued, "And what is that?"

With a straight face, he indicated her generous cleavage.

"With a body like that, you wouldn't be mistaken for a rocket scientist."

Eldon was now choking in the throes of some kind of apoplectic fit but Jay didn't notice.

His attention was all on the flame-haired wench he intended to get to know better. Intimately, in fact. Repeatedly. One night wouldn't be nearly enough. Eternity might not be long enough to realize the promise of passion in those sweet lips.

"I see. You want to know my price?" She considered him for a moment, her face unreadable. "One million dollars."

Jay made the mistake of laughing again.

"Annually," she added sweetly.

She was funnier than he was, he thought in envy. Amazing. All that, and a sense of humor, too.

"A million dollars?" He kidded back. "You must be some kind of specialist."

She nodded graciously. "Yes, I am. Lyle is very generous but one million would top the standing offer NASA made me."

For the first time, Jay sensed that something had gone wrong somewhere.

"NASA?"

His formerly sniggering cohorts were cautiously shuffling away.

"Yes. You've heard of it, haven't you?" Sympathy glimmered in her violet eyes. "The letters are an acronym. That means a word made up of initials," she explained in the tolerant voice one might use on the mentally deficient or the very young.

"It stands for the National Aeronautics and—"

"I know what it stands for," Jay broke in. "Now why would a nice group of letters like that make an offer to a woman like you?"

He thought there must be all kinds of hidden benefits to federal funding.

"Well." She colored prettily and cast a humble glance down at her shoes. "They'd make me an offer like that because I am a specialist. An interior ballistics specialist." She blinked thickly lashed violet eyes at him, the picture of innocence, just before she delivered the topper. "A rocket scientist."

"You're not." The denial escaped him unthinkingly.

"Oh, I'm afraid I am. So unless you're willing to make me an offer like that, then we don't have anything to discuss."

"Grant doesn't pay you a million a year," Jay accused.

He knew it for a fact. He'd seen the figures himself. He was now in charge of marketing and he'd spent the past week with Eldon going over the company's financial picture in detail. He didn't know her name but nobody had a salary in that range.

Then it struck him: A. Leslie. The elusive, reclusive research scientist. The bombshell was A. Leslie.

He'd expected A. Leslie to be a man.

Thank God she wasn't.

In her own sweet time, Miss Firecracker responded to his statement. "No, he doesn't," she agreed. "But that is what you'd have to pay me to work for a patronizing, hormone-ruled, IQ deficient, arrogant and mannerless cretin with delusions of self-importance like you."

Her honeyed voice never rose a decibel. That her words crashed over him like thunder was some kind of auditory illusion.

He'd never been insulted so thoroughly. And so politely. Another of her impressive accomplishments.

"Nice to meet you, Mr. Whitman. Now I know who to avoid."

Having delivered her parting shot, the fatal beauty turned on her magnificent heels and walked away.

Jay gazed with rapture at her retreating back. From any angle, she was something to see. She had the body of a goddess, an amazing sense of humor, great taste in clothes, enough brains, evidently, to compete with Einstein's memory.

And some kind of natural chemistry.

He tingled all over from the charge of merely standing next to her. He could imagine the fires she'd ignite with one touch.

He was entranced.

He was on fire.

He was in love.

He gazed after her with something approaching worship and declared prayerfully, "What a woman."

Beside him, the accountant was practically weeping.

"Now you've done it. You insulted her. You called her a-a—" Eldon couldn't bring himself to even say it. He rounded on Jay, completely overwrought, and clutched his lapels wildly. "Do you know what you've done? She invented the Golden Galaxy. The Screaming Scarlet Siren. The Fantasy Fountain." Eldon listed her credits with rising hysteria.

The first vague hint of alarm stirred.

"You're talking about our best sellers," Jay observed.

Eldon nodded so vigorously that Jay feared whiplash.

"Yes! That's what I've been trying to tell you! She's the head of R&D, Frontier's resident wizard. She's Grant's pet and he'll do anything to keep her happy, including replacing a certain vice-president with—what did she call it? Delusions of self-importance? Her creations have put Frontier on top and Grant knows it."

Eldon having hysterics looked something like Elmer Fudd on speed, Jay thought. The man was trembling, wire-rimmed glasses askew, normally straight and neat hair sticking out at all angles, his eyes wild.

"Eldon, Eldon. Relax," Jay said in an effort to calm the overwrought accountant.

"Relax? I can't relax. What if she quits? What if she goes to the competition and takes her patents with her?"

Eldon was rough on tuxedo jackets, Jay mused.

"Come on, calm down. What's this about patents?" He asked the question in an attempt to steer the conversation into more quiet waters.

The accountant released Jay's thoroughly subdued lapels and ran shaking hands through his pale hair, smoothing down the worst of the cowlicks.

"The deal she has says that she holds the patents to anything that she invents. In return, she grants Frontier exclusive rights to develop her brainchildren. It's a clause that protects her from losing on profits she's rightfully entitled to and protects Frontier from paying for R&D facilities to advance competitors," Eldon explained.

Jay thought that over for a moment.

"So she couldn't take anything to a competitor, then, right? Because Frontier has exclusive rights to the work she's done here?"

Eldon calmed visibly, considering that. "Yes. Right. But losing her new work would be just as bad," he added unhappily. He gazed mournfully after the redhead as if watching a dream drift away and crumble to dust. "She was making a new blue this year."

Jay didn't even try to make sense of that mysterious remark.

"I think you're worrying about nothing. She doesn't seem all that upset to me," he pointed out in soothing tones.

As a matter of fact, he thought she looked like she was having fun, drinking champagne and dancing.

If she wanted to have fun, he was the one she wanted. He was a good time on legs. And off them, if he could persuade her to explore the possibilities.

In fact, the more he thought about it, the more certain Jay became that it was his duty to the company to entertain the resident wizard. And certainly he owed it to her to rescue her from the unwanted attentions of other men.

"I think I'll go ask her to dance."

Eldon stared at him as if he'd lost his mind.

"I don't think she likes you," he informed Jay.

"Of course she does." Confidence oozed from every pore as Jay boasted, "She made eye contact. She came over to meet me. She was standing close."

Eldon gaped at him for a moment in stunned silence before cautiously repeating, "I really don't think she likes you."

With a pitying glance at the man, Jay explained, "You just don't understand women."

"She called you names. She said you'd have to pay her a million dollars to put up with you."

Oh, yes, she had. She had spirit. The thought warmed his already heated blood.

"I know." Jay smiled cheerfully. "She's playing hard to get."

Eldon gazed at him in palpable doubt. "What makes you say that?"

"Elementary, my dear Eldon. Consider what she evidently spends her days playing with," Jay suggested.

Eldon considered. "Explosives?"

Jay shot the man an impatient look. "No. Rockets, Eldon. And rockets, my friend, are widely recognized as phallic symbols of the most potent order."

Eldon gasped. "You mean—"

"I mean," Jay interrupted smoothly, "I think it's time she dedicated some research to the real thing. Eldon, I've decided to give my body to science."

Eldon let out a low sound of despair.

He gazed after Jay's departing back with a doomed expression on his face.

Anna was fox-trotting with Bill Whittaker, who seemed to have recovered from his initial shock, when the obnoxious man who wanted to be her "patron" cut in.

She was still fuming over his insulting comments and for a moment she actually considered leaving him stranded on the dance floor. But that would be running away and she was determined to stand up for herself and confront trouble head-on.

She would not be bullied by him.

If she backed down, she'd be setting a bad precedent and she'd have only herself to blame if the work relationship caused her problems. That he worked for Frontier in some capacity was obvious. She couldn't hope to avoid him. In fact, it was surprising that they hadn't met sooner.

He was the kind of man others looked up to, a natural leader. He'd had that group of testosterone junkies hanging on his every word.

If she was going to have to deal with him, she might as well start now. So she called on reserves of patience she hadn't known she possessed and graciously continued the dance with her new partner.

If he gave her any trouble, she could always wield her stiletto heels on his feet. The leather dress shoes he wore looked rather thin.

"So you're the elusive A. Leslie," the tall, dark and obnoxious stranger commented. His hungry ebony gaze took her in, surveying the effect of her red-on-red ensemble.

"That's right." Anna kept her tone carefully neutral. She would *not* be provoked.

"Well, A. Leslie, if you always look this good, I can see why you stay out of sight. Productivity would grind to a halt." The insufferable lecher grinned at her, obviously highly entertained by his own scintillating wit.

"Thank you."

The sarcasm was evidently wasted on him, however. He appeared to take her reply as encouragement.

"No, thank you." His smile broadened, a feat she wouldn't have thought possible, and he tightened his hold on her as he continued, "That's some dress you're almost wearing. I hope your last dance partner doesn't have a history of heart trouble."

She looked at him in suspicion.

He looked back at her in lustful anticipation.

"Since you're a rocket scientist, it seems appropriate that you have one heavenly body."

He drew her even closer and continued, "Did I tell you how happy I am to meet you?"

It was embarrassingly obvious to Anna that at least one part of him was very happy to meet her, indeed. And inappropriate as it was, his interest sparked her own. There was something about his nearness, his sheer relentless sexual confidence, that planted ideas in her gonads, if not her head.

She tried to pull away slightly in an attempt to salvage the situation and to stop the unwanted sensation of heat curling through her abdomen.

Jay gripped her satin-covered waist and molded her fully against him. Heat built from every point of contact and contracted into a hungry throb.

This had to stop.

Anna placed the lethal heel of her lovely new red pump on top of his foot and ruthlessly ground down. His shoes proved to be as inadequate against attack as they looked and with a startled yelp, he stumbled and lost his hold.

"Sorry," Anna murmured, completely unrepentant. "I guess it was an accident. Like the way you accidentally got a little out of line."

Unbelievably, admiration instead of contrition or even a hint of dismay gleamed in his dark eyes.

"Whoa. You're one dangerous bundle of love."

"Mr. Whitman, I would appreciate it if you didn't refer to me as a bundle of love, or any other little endearments you have in mind. We work for the same company." Firmly, Anna took the bull by the horns and asserted herself.

"Don't tell me you have a rule against mixing business and pleasure?" Mock horror lit the overly handsome face that nature may have intended as consolation for the vacuum behind it.

He'd certainly been shortchanged in the wits he nevertheless seemed so fond of, Anna thought sourly. She was attracted to a cretin. It must be nature's law of balance in effect, seeking intellectual equilibrium in their offspring.

He gave up on impressing her with the evidence of his virility in favor of showing off his dancing skills as he led her through a series of flashy steps, ending with a deep dip.

As he bent over her, he winked and offered, "Why don't we cut to the chase. My place or yours?"

Before she could answer that, he returned her to an upright position and spun her expertly in a move that brought her hard against him, trapped by his long arms.

"You feel what's happening between us. I know you do."

Seductively, he back-stepped and took her with him, plastered against his front.

She certainly did feel it and it was beyond her social skills to cope with. Of all times for her libido to decide to wake up and pay attention, this had to be the worst. "Ah, Mr. Whitman," Anna began, only to be cut off.

"Jay," he corrected with a wolfish flash of white teeth. "You can hardly call me Mr. Whitman. It would sound ridiculous."

He nuzzled her cheek and murmured naughtily in her ear, "Harder, Mr. Whitman. Yes, Mr. Whitman. Deeper. Oh, Mr. Whitman!"

Anna nearly choked.

He smiled at her innocently. "You see? It doesn't work."

Clearly, she needed more time with her new research project. Anna was completely out of her depth in this area of communication.

Then she recovered her determination.

No. She wasn't going to hold back any more.

She was the bold, confident woman in the red dress she'd seen in the store mirror. She was comfortable with her body. Secure in her sexuality. Sure of herself and her value, as a woman, as a person, as an individual.

She'd struck Lyle speechless.

She could handle one leering, libidinous lunatic.

"Hmm. I'm not sure," Anna mused, dancing closer and nestling her generous curves against his male length. A treacherous wave of heat and weakness struck her at the intimate contact but she had a goal and she stuck to it. Her mouth was level with his ear and she murmured into it, "Oh, Mr. Whitman. Oh, yes, Mr. Whitman. Like that. Deeper, Mr. Whitman. Oh, yes! Yes!"

Thoroughly enjoying herself now, she groaned with feeling, "Oh, my God, Mr. Whitman."

It shut him up, she noted in delight. He was staring at her with glazed eyes and his breathing had grown labored.

"Do you like it like that, Mr. Whitman?" She nipped at his earlobe to be sure she had his complete attention.

A shudder ran through his lanky frame.

"Or is this better? Jay. Jay, I want you. Now, Jay," she begged sweetly and blew in his ear for good measure. "Oh, yes, Jay. Take me. Take me to the stars."

His eyes darkened even further with desire and he promised hoarsely, "I will, honey, I will."

Anna placed one manicured fingertip against his lower lip and slowly, regretfully shook her head.

"No, I'm afraid not."

"Why not?" he asked against her fingertip with a persuasive kiss.

"Oh, Mr. Whitman. You can't take me to the stars." Wickedly, Anna let her body brush tantalizingly against his as she spoke. Tender hands framed his face and she rubbed her nose against his in a teasing gesture, continuing, "You wouldn't know how to calculate the escape velocity. You aren't a rocket scientist."

With a theatrical sigh of regret for what might have been, she turned and strolled away, leaving her thoroughly defeated adversary behind.

Which was harder than it should have been.

Chapter Three

Anna was still surging with energy from the sexual skirmish when she reached the elevators and pressed the down button with unnecessary force.

She nearly jumped when a tentative voice behind her called a faint, "Excuse me."

She whirled, ready to resume battle.

And relaxed. It wasn't *him*. Which she should have known, from the polite greeting. *He* didn't know the meaning of polite. It was a totally foreign concept. Of course, if Jay Whitman had been polite she would never have felt the force of his masculine interest and she wouldn't be feeling an unaccustomed thrill of feminine power in response now.

The man before her wasn't her overbearing, under-brained, fast-talking nemesis. It was the bespectacled, polite head accountant.

"Hello, Eldon."

"Hello, Miss Fire—I mean, uh," Eldon stammered and ground to a halt.

"It's all right, Eldon. I knew about the nickname. Jane told me," she assured the nervous man.

"Oh. That's good." He paused and blushed. "Uh, I just wanted to tell you…" he sucked in a deep breath, focused his eyes somewhere to her left and spat out in a rush, "nobody thought there was anything— That you were—were—"

"Eldon," she broke in kindly as he floundered again, "it's all right. I'm not upset with you."

He seemed to sag with relief.

Anna went on, "I think Mr. Whitman is a little bit of a clown and just got carried away. I'm certain that he wouldn't deliberately undermine a colleague's credibility or reputation."

There, she thought in satisfaction. Killing with kindness. If she refused to acknowledge any insult, the insulter was frustrated in the attempt.

She rather enjoyed the idea of frustrating her nemesis further. Still, it was terribly sweet of Eldon to be so concerned about her that he followed her to apologize for something he hadn't even done.

Who knew how many friends she'd missed out on all this time she'd been hiding herself away, buried in work? To her surprise, she'd really enjoyed the party tonight. Most of her coworkers had been glad to speak with her. In the three years she'd been with Frontier, she'd proven her ability and her value. Yes, some archaic attitudes still lingered but that was her own fault for not making it a point to bang heads together sooner.

A soft chime indicated the arrival of an elevator car and the doors slid open a moment later.

"Well, that's mine. I want to get an early start in the morning." Anna smiled warmly at the serious man and stepped into the elevator. "Good night, Eldon."

"Good night," he answered faintly. For a moment, he looked as if he wanted to say something more. Then he waved and returned to the party as the doors slid shut.

It was a short ride down.

Not nearly long enough to sort out the incredible events of the day and evening.

Anna smiled, remembering the sheer fun of getting one up on Lyle and rendering him speechless. She'd led him around by his bowtie and threatened to garrote him with it.

She'd come right back at a certain black-haired bad boy and given as good as she got.

Her smile widened at the thought of how she'd left him. Maybe she'd given better. Certainly his left shoe would never be the same. And where had she gotten the nerve to talk dirty to him until he was stunned into silence? Let alone thought on her feet fast enough to come up with the punch line?

She thought Jane would be proud.

She certainly was. It felt really good to stand up for herself, to ask for what she wanted, to throw a verbal gauntlet back with a twist instead of quietly taking it.

Anna stepped out of the elevator and headed to the front of the building where her rented limo waited. As she walked, she hummed an old protest tune about hearing women roar.

The driver saw her coming and moved the car closer to the sidewalk so she wouldn't get her shoes muddy. He got out to open her door and help her in and Anna reveled in the service.

That he was young, muscular and handsome in a square-jawed sort of way didn't hurt, either.

"Thank you," she said warmly, meeting his blue eyes directly and the man smiled back.

"You're welcome," he assured her, before returning to his seat and taking the wheel.

Anna left the window separating the front from the back open and the friendly chauffeur, whose name was Tom, started up a cheerful conversation on the way to her home.

"How was your party?"

Anna smiled again as she answered, "Wonderful."

It was true. She'd had fun, even while tangling with a certain adversary on the dance floor. Maybe even especially then.

They talked about the mud, the long winter and spring fever. Anna marveled that she was actually exchanging small talk painlessly. Before, if she'd ever thought to rent a limousine, she certainly wouldn't have chatted with the driver. And she would have missed out on an enjoyable conversation with a charming and interesting man.

The talk turned to movies and Anna mentioned that an old friend had done the detonations for a current action hit.

"No kidding!" Tom met her eyes in the rearview mirror, his face alight with admiration. "I've wanted to see that. I heard they blow up a bridge, an oil tanker and three cars. Is that what you do?"

"Oh, no, if I make a bomb, it's an accident," she answered. "I only do fireworks."

He was visibly disappointed and Anna hid a smile at his reaction. The Golden Galaxy just wasn't a sufficiently testosterone-laden explosion, she guessed.

Then to her surprise he asked her if she wanted to go see it with him. *A date?* How did she handle this, she wondered.

While she was deciding, he spoke again.

"Hey, I'm sorry, I shouldn't have asked."

"No, it's all right," Anna assured him. "I just haven't been out much for a while. I'm only starting to get back into circulation."

He gave an understanding nod. "Bad breakup, huh? Those really hurt."

A breakup? No, it was a lot worse than that. She wasn't just getting back into circulation, she'd never been *in* circulation. She hadn't had any relationships, good or bad. She was a twenty-eight-year-old virgin, which probably made her some kind of endangered species.

The limo arrived at her townhouse. Tom quickly helped Anna out again and ushered her to her front door.

"Don't worry, you'll be ready for somebody else before you know it. Take your time easing into things and spend time with your friends. That's what always gets me through."

Anna thanked him for the advice and gave him a farewell wave, then went in and shut the door before she started to laugh.

What next? The new, improved Anna was finding life was full of surprises. Relationship advice from her chauffeur. An offer for a date.

Now that was something she really should think about, she decided. The new Anna was evidently more approachable and would get asked out again.

She hadn't set out to practice celibacy deliberately. It had just sort of happened that way. As a teenager, she'd been too tall and awkward to appeal to the opposite sex. Combined with a reputation as a brain and an innate reserve, it hadn't exactly set her up for an active social life.

Then the ugly duckling had abruptly transformed into a swan and she hadn't trusted the sudden surge of interest in her from boys who'd always been indifferent.

She'd been caught off guard and unprepared, so she'd just said no to everybody.

She guessed her family had sort of prepared the way, too. The opposite of the Jane's close-knit, loving family, hers was distant and cool. She'd always felt vaguely out of place at home and by the time she'd left, she'd established the loner habit.

Between schoolwork, which she'd buried herself in, and work, moving away from old friends and starting over with no ties, it had been easy to keep on hiding away from life.

Still, maybe there was hope for her. Jay Whitman had really thought she was an experienced woman of the world. Or of the night. Whatever. And thanks to a movie Jane had rented and made her watch, she knew how to fake a good, passionate moan.

It was a start.

Certainly it had been enough to floor one loud-mouthed man.

Anna removed her shoes and padded over the soft beige carpet to the stairs that led to her bedroom. The multilevel design had a garage with a laundry and storage area on the ground floor, the main living area on the second and two bedrooms and a bath on the top floor.

As she walked through, Anna took a good, close look at her living space and decided that she was living like a nun in more ways than one.

That was something else that was going to change.

No pictures hung on the bare walls. Only the African violets on a couple of windowsills and the odd hanging fern softened the Early Hotel look. Even her refrigerator was bare, except for a snapshot of her from Christmas with Jane and the rest of the Millers and a grocery list.

No clutter on the smoothly polished tabletops or empty, gleaming counters.

Looking around her, Anna had a sudden wild urge to throw something, anything, even her clothing, all over the place just to prove that somebody lived here.

It wasn't an unattractive place, exactly, she decided. Just…lifeless. It needed some color. Some personality. The neutral color scheme was nice enough and some colorful throw pillows and maybe curtains would do a lot to brighten things up. She made a mental note to talk to Jane about it and ask for ideas.

She needed some pictures, too. A Van Gogh print, maybe. One of the sunflower series or "Starry Night". She'd always liked that skyscape.

Redecorating would be easy. Figuring out how to navigate the perilous dating waters, however, might take a little more thought and effort. She was a total beginner. Going places with John as her escort didn't count. He would no more come on to her than he would if she were really his sister.

What she needed, Anna mused, was some experience.

She hadn't exactly been living in a complete vacuum. She knew about the basic facts of life. About biology and birth control and disease prevention. She knew that it was okay to ask a man out and even to request a sexual history and blood test, although it sounded terribly unappealing.

She just didn't know about the feelings.

When it came to the world of emotions, her ignorance and inexperience were truly vast.

What would it feel like, Anna wondered, to fall in love? To passionately and intensely desire a man? Seeing movies, reading about it and talking to Jane about her love life only went so far. Anna was too good a researcher not to know that sometimes a huge distance existed between theory and practical application.

What did she want? That was really the question.

She pondered it as she removed her makeup and brushed out hair that fell in loose waves to her waist.

What she wanted was to grow as a person. To find out what her needs and desires were. To explore her sexuality.

She wanted to stop hiding away in the world of carefully controlled, methodically researched science. She wanted to find outlets for her long-buried emotions before they shriveled up and died.

Anna reflected for the first time that she might have been drawn to focusing on fireworks because they represented a form of artistic expression and so provided an emotional release of sorts.

As far as today went, she'd gotten off to a good start, she decided.

Today, she'd been daring and feminine and to her surprise, the change was a welcome one, and not just to herself.

A whole world full of possibilities and people, potential friends and potential dates included, waited for her. It had been there all along. She just hadn't seen it or known how to reach out.

Well, it was midnight and the ball was over but Cinderella wasn't going to go back to the kitchen to take a load of crap from her ungrateful family while she waited for some prince to get a clue.

No, Anna decided firmly, she was going to get some sleep so she'd be ready to roar again tomorrow.

And at work, she'd tackle the search for the salt or powdered metal that, when combined with fuel and an oxidizer, would give off a brilliant blue that would work for her planned red, white and blue finale.

Also, Jane would be dying to hear all about the party. She'd probably already heard about Mr. Tall, Dark and Too-Mouthy-To-Be-So-Handsome Whitman, if she hadn't actually met him yet. Anna wondered why she didn't remember Jane mentioning anybody new.

Well, whatever else the next day might have in store, she had the distinct feeling that she hadn't heard the last of Jay.

A man with a mouth like that would be used to getting the last word.

Jay wasn't getting the last word the following morning.

In fact, the way things were going he didn't think he'd ever get even one word in edgewise.

Lyle Grant certainly knew how to give a lecture.

Jay wondered if he'd ever been a drill sergeant.

The minute he'd arrived in his office, he'd been summoned by Grant's secretary. Now he found himself standing uncomfortably in front of a very long, very heavy mahogany desk, getting raked over the coals almost as well as Miss Firecracker could do it.

But she did it so much more enjoyably, he thought wistfully.

The red-hot redhead was also infinitely easier on the eyes.

It seemed ludicrous that Grant was chewing him up and spitting him out on her behalf when she'd done such an admirable job all by herself already. She'd done it with style, too.

She'd smiled innocently at him while grinding her heel through his foot. She'd talked dirty to him with an enthusiasm worthy of a 900 telephone number operator. And she'd blown in his ear.

She was the most amazing woman he'd ever met and that was saying something.

He'd met an awful lot of women.

Just thinking about her made his heart sing and made his body start a long, slow burn. It was heavenly torment. He couldn't wait to see her again. The very thought made him smile.

"What do you have to smile about, that's what I'd like to know," Lyle barked. "I'm not smiling. Do you see me smiling?"

"No, I—"

"You're damned right I'm not and I'll tell you why. You upset Anna." Lyle cut him off to cut him down some more. He glowered fiercely at Jay and puffed on his cigar.

Jay had a sudden mind picture of cartoon puffs of smoke rolling out the man's ears instead of his mouth.

Then his attention turned to what he'd said. Anna. Jay tasted the name mentally. Yes, it fit her, he decided. A strong name for a strong woman. Much better than the bland and asexual A. Leslie. Anna was far from bland or asexual. She was all woman and she deserved a fitting name.

"Now I'm going to explain how things work around here," Lyle glowered and puffed some more. "Here at Frontier, we all have our place. We all have our job to do. We all have our own function. I'm the heart of the company."

He paused to let that sink in.

"She's the brains."

Another pause.

"And you are what I'd call the helping hands. Do I make myself clear?" A penetrating stare accompanied the question.

Jay figured now he'd get to respond. "Yes, I see—"

"No, I don't think you do see," Grant cut in again, proving Jay wrong. "I think you need to understand what Anna means to Frontier."

Jay needed to understand what Anna meant to him.

He wanted to make her laugh.

He wanted to dance with her again. She danced like a dream and he was glad he'd lost a bet that landed him in ballroom dancing lessons. He wanted to be Fred to her Ginger.

In fact, he just plain wanted her in a peculiar way that involved his mind and heart as well as his body.

Did she feel the same emotional pull toward him? The physical attraction was undeniable, at least. She couldn't possibly be indifferent to him. She had to feel something. True, he'd made a mess of things, gotten them off on the wrong foot by planting it firmly in his mouth when she introduced herself, but then again, he supposed she was used to turning men into blithering idiots on the first meeting. Probably well into the second and third meetings, too.

The only way to find out, Jay decided happily, was to see her again. As soon as possible. Again and again, in fact.

With some difficulty, he picked up the thread of the lecture he was supposed to be listening to.

"She's a genius, son. A pyrotechnic wizard. Her inventions are what made this company what it is. We were a dime-store operation before she came in," Lyle continued to verbally barrel along, blowing smoke in amazing quantities.

A dime-store operation? Actually, that was an exaggeration but Jay let it slide in the spirit of charity. He appreciated the sentiment. In fact, however, Frontier had been in a position to expand and Anna had been recruited in a carefully planned move. But if she hadn't gone for it, Grant would have found somebody else. Jay could agree, though, that nobody else would add quite what she did.

Any woman who could wear a dress like the one she'd worn last night deserved all the praise Grant wanted to heap on her.

Jay felt like singing her praises, himself.

He concentrated as Lyle went on, "She could have gone anywhere. She could have gone to NASA."

So she hadn't been kidding about that.

"She came here. And she'll stay here as long as she's happy." Grant fixed him with another cold, hard stare. "I intend to keep her happy. Understand me?"

"Yes, I—"

Jay found himself cut off once again as the man continued, "Let me explain something to you."

Pause. Puff.

Jay didn't even try to speak. He was getting wise to the man's tricks. Instead, he patiently waited for the other shoe to drop.

Grant drew deeply on his cigar and stated, "Nearly everything she does could have some military application. The Apollo spacecraft alone used over two hundred pyrotechnic devices, all designed by artists like her."

He stabbed his cigar at Jay for emphasis and went on, "Luckily for us, she wanted to make pretty fireworks more than she wanted to work on rocket ships."

Good God, she really was a rocket scientist, Jay thought in shock. Not that he hadn't believed her. He just hadn't seen any obvious connection between the waves of color that lit up the Fourth of July and the impressive launching of an Apollo rocket.

"Maybe now you're beginning to get the picture." Lyle sat back and eyed his silenced audience. He had the boy's complete attention now, he thought with satisfaction. Now it was time to build him up a little after yanking the rug out from underneath him.

Lyle thought of Frontier as more of a big family than anything else. A patriarchy, with himself as the undisputed head. His boy had needed a spanking but now he thought he was ready to be reasonable.

"Now, son, I don't want you to think I don't appreciate what you have to offer." Lyle spoke in a kinder, gentler tone and drew another taste of Cuba. "I know without a good man in marketing this company will never realize its potential. That's where you come in. Your solid business sense will help us capitalize on our assets and guide our growth."

He paused again for effect.

"Now that means working together with everybody in a team effort. Anna's a key player and I want you to get along with her. Understand?"

"Yes, I think I do." Jay nodded.

"Good. Now get going and go bury the hatchet. And not in each other."

"Yes, sir." The other man headed out the door with an air of determination that had Lyle smiling at his departing back.

Whitman was working out perfectly.

He'd meant every word he said. He wanted Anna happy. He didn't call burying herself alive and working all hours happy. Not by a long shot.

What she needed was some romance. Passion. Fireworks of a different kind. Jay was just the man for the job. There'd been enough sparks flying between them last night to create a fire hazard.

It couldn't have gone better.

Yes, he mused, bringing Whitman in was a good move, all the way around. He was the kind of man Frontier's marketing and financial management needed. If that same man wasn't also just what Anna needed, he'd eat his cigar.

Lyle eased his chair back, propped his feet on his desk and puffed in quiet contentment.

Until a telling cloud of scarlet smoke came from nowhere and filled the office.

Chapter Four

Jane deposited one cup of tea on the desk and challenged, "Talk."

Anna glanced up from behind her stack of books and tried an innocent, befuddled expression. "About what?"

That got her an impatient look from her fuming assistant. Jane started tapping her toe expectantly.

Anna gave it up. When Jane started tapping her toe, it meant she was going to drag it all out of her one way or another. Besides, for once she really had something juicy to gossip about.

She threw up her hands as if to ward off Jane's evil eye.

"Okay, okay! I went to the party. I wore the most fabulous red dress you've ever seen or heard of. I told Lyle I wanted a better parking spot, without mud, and this morning there it was!" Anna sat back, glowing with pleasure. As a matter of fact, he'd done even better than she'd asked. He'd put up a nice little placard with her name on it to mark her space.

She'd been glowing since the night before, actually. Her new attitude suited her. A little bit of badness was good for the soul, evidently. When she'd looked in the mirror to do her makeup, she'd seen violet eyes sparkling with life. Even her hair seemed to crackle with vibrant energy within the confines of the practical braid she wore.

Speaking of being bad, Anna decided she'd better warn Jane about the little trick she'd just pulled.

"Oh, and I detonated a little smoking something in Lyle's office a little bit ago, so if he comes down here hollering and lecturing, you'll know why. Be sure he doesn't bring a cigar with him into the lab, though."

Jane gasped. "No. You didn't. You did! I can't believe it." Laughter bubbled from the dark-haired girl at the thought of the demure and dignified head of research running amok and playing mad scientist. "I always knew you had it in you!" she cheered and jumped up to offer a victory hug.

"Thank you, Jane, you're a true friend." Anna was fairly bouncing in her seat. She really couldn't remember when she'd had as much fun.

"I guess you were right about the shrink," the brunette admitted.

"No, actually, you were. I decided I didn't need one," Anna answered solemnly.

"Ah ha! So what's all this, then?" Jane waved at the pile of books on Anna's desk.

"Books."

Jane rolled her eyes in exasperation at the evasive response.

"Okay, okay. Books on communication, assertiveness and the differences between men and women. Relationship stuff," Anna replied.

Jane's eyes widened further.

"You're kidding. I don't believe it! You're reading up on men and women stuff? As in, getting ready for dating stuff? As in, plunging into the world of romance?"

Anna grinned back at her friend. "Well, I thought it was about time."

"Ha! I thought you weren't interested in time. Not your field and all that."

Anna put on her best serious, studious expression.

"Time is a dimension, not a field."

Jane groaned in mock agony at the poor joke.

"That's really bad," she accused.

"Well, so am I. As of yesterday. The new me is bad, bad, bad and I couldn't be better," Anna announced. The satisfaction in her voice spoke volumes.

Jane took a closer look at the books. "A guide to being bad?" She raised a brow in appraisal, folded her arms across her chest and inquired, "Okay, now what gives? What did you do, Anna?"

"Yes, what did you do, Anna?" A mocking, masculine voice chimed in, startling both women.

The source of the voice leaned casually in the doorway in a pose that would have done GQ proud. It artfully displayed the gray wool suit to advantage, which in turn displayed a long, tall male body to advantage.

Unfair, really, Anna thought. That body had enough natural advantages without the model pose and stylish suit.

Her eyes traveled up to the dark eyes that set off the too-handsome face under jet-black hair.

It was him.

Anna sighed inwardly. Just her luck. Then again, she'd just known he'd be back to try and get the last word. No doubt he'd spent the night thinking up new and better insults.

Well, maybe the best defense was a good offense, in this case. She loaded her verbal ammunition and fired the first shot.

"Ahh, yes, Mr. Whitman, the not-so-missing link. Why are you here?"

His glowing eyes warmed further, if that was possible. "I came to see if you missed me. Did you miss me, Anna?"

Anna stared back at him in silence.

Jane's eyes silently begged her for details.

Casually, Jay unwrapped himself from the doorjamb and strolled over to take a look at Anna's reading material. He perused the titles, then slanted a look at her.

"Honey, if you want to do a little research on the differences between men and women, I'll be happy to volunteer as your star subject." He winked and added naughtily, "I'll show you mine if you'll show me yours."

Anna scowled at her unwanted visitor. "I don't want to see yours."

"Are you sure? That isn't what you said last night when you blew in my ear," Jay observed.

At that, Jane's eyebrows shot up and vanished beneath her bangs.

Her look of amazement deepened when Jay turned his gleaming black eyes on her and informed her, "She's crazy about me."

Anna rammed his side with her elbow, since it was conveniently within reach. "That would make me just plain crazy."

"She likes to play rough, too," the irrepressible scoundrel continued in a voice that plainly said he liked it that way. "She's dangerous. She already has me limping."

"Is that what's keeping you from leaving?" Anna asked, sweet as poison.

He turned back to her and shook his head in mock dismay.

"Come on, you can't try to hide something like this. An office romance never stays a secret and in our case it's likely to make headlines. So be nice and give me a kiss."

The outrageous flirt dared her with his wicked eyes while he offered her his sexy mouth.

Anna stared back and refused to respond.

Undeterred, he shrugged and said, "Okay, you can kiss me later. But don't blame me if we get caught in the elevator."

He poked through her books some more and pulled out the guide to becoming a bad girl.

He tutted and wagged a finger at her. "Now here's something you don't need. But if you do want to be bad, little girl, I'm ready, willing and able to help." The innuendo in his voice was heavy enough to fell a bull moose.

Anna pushed him back and peered around him to catch her assistant's eye. "Jane, would you mind excusing us for a minute?"

"Make that at least ten. Maybe fifteen." Jay thoughtfully eyed the desktop, then the counter space as if considering the amorous possibilities. "Better yet, let's go to a little hotel I know."

Anna glared. "We're not going to a hotel."

Jay looked deeply disappointed. "A real bad girl would. A really, really bad one would suggest it."

"I'll just go run those copies down the hall," Jane offered. She scooped a sheaf of papers off the photocopier by her desk to corroborate the excuse. As she left, she mouthed, 'I want to know everything' behind Jay's back. She disappeared and closed the door behind her.

"Nice girl," Jay observed. "Thoughtful, too."

Then he turned back to her and moved closer until he had Anna pinned in her chair.

"You didn't answer me. Did you miss me?"

"If I say yes, will you go away?"

"I don't know. Say 'yes'," Jay suggested as he pretended to consider the question. "I think I'd like to hear that, anyway. The way you said it last night."

"Yes."

The clipped, sarcastic tone was a world away from a breathy, impassioned moan of sensual longing.

He gave her an impatient look. "No, that won't work. You'll have to kiss me, instead."

His lips closed over hers with warm persuasion and Anna felt a distinct tingling sensation that spread from her lips to a point low in her belly, leaving heat and a hunger for closer contact in its wake.

Soft, tempting nibbles tasted the full curve of her mouth in a slow, thorough exploration. With a low groan, Jay wrapped her long braid around his hand and used it to pull her closer. Then he stroked her lips with his tongue.

Anna partly opened her mouth to protest and he took advantage of the moment to swirl inside and taste her deeply.

So this was a French kiss, Anna thought in shock. He had his tongue in her mouth and was coaxing hers to play.

It was research, after all, she reminded herself. He'd offered to be a subject himself.

She gave him her tongue.

Then she wasn't really sure what happened but somehow they were on her desk and he was laying half on top of her. His deep, wet kisses were getting hotter and hotter and her books fell to the floor with a crash.

The sound penetrated the sensual haze clouding Anna's mind and startled her to awareness. This experiment had clearly gotten a little out of hand. She started to struggle under his weight.

Dazed, Jay recognized her withdrawal and lifted his head. Impassioned black eyes bore into amethyst depths. "My God," he grated in a hoarse whisper, "I knew you were good."

Anna didn't know what to say to that, so she didn't say anything. Instead, she touched a tentative tongue to suddenly dry lips.

Jay groaned at the sight and took her mouth again in a thoroughly seductive kiss, penetrating her velvet lips with his tongue in slow, thrusting strokes.

Anna didn't know what might have happened next if Jane hadn't come back in and cleared her throat.

She looked up in shock at her amused assistant.

"Uh, maybe I should have made it twenty?" Jane asked meekly, trying to suppress the smile that tugged at the corner of her mouth.

Anna turned her blank, somewhat wild stare on Jay. What had happened? Had she actually been passionately necking with the mouthy man for fifteen minutes? On one level, Anna decided it was good to know that his mouth was good for something besides verbal skirmishes.

Jay stared just as blankly back at her. Then he helped her up.

"I'll be back to pick you up for lunch," he stated in a flat voice.

Then he kissed her again. Hard.

His black eyes mesmerized hers as he added, "Make it a long lunch."

He turned and walked to the door, then suddenly came back and gave Anna one last brief, hard kiss, as if acting under some sort of mysterious compulsion.

"Nice to meet you," Jay added to the stunned Jane on his way out.

Anna watched him go, still in a daze. Then she collapsed onto her chair and pleaded, "Tea. I need tea."

Jane complied then took the seat across from her again.

"Okay, boss, what gives here? You obviously didn't tell me something about last night."

Anna waved a vague hand in her direction in a silent play for time. She had to compose herself. She picked up her cup and took a hasty gulp of the herbal concoction. She hoped it would restore her to her senses.

It did help. The chamomile blend was soothing, as always. She hoped it would work quickly to soothe the stunning confusion the obnoxious man had left behind. He'd probably kissed her just to get back at her for blowing in his ear and getting the last word last night.

They were even now. He'd definitely gotten the last word, although Anna had no idea what it was. Maybe it would come to her later.

Everything after his tongue touched hers was a kaleidoscopic blur.

She took another swallow of her tea and managed to answer Jane, who was being remarkably patient.

"Well. There really isn't much to tell."

Jane let out an unladylike snort of disbelief. "Not much to tell? You were inches from making it on your desk with an incredibly sexy man just minutes ago. And he says you blew in his ear last night and asked him to show you his." The brunette paused and eyed her friend for telltale signs of heavy drinking. "You weren't wearing a lampshade on your head or anything like that, were you?"

Anna swallowed some tea the wrong way and coughed. When she recovered, she answered, "No. I had some champagne, that's all."

"Uh-huh." Jane's doubt was evident.

"No, really. I was perfectly sober when I rubbed my body all over his and blew in his ear."

Now it was Jane's turn to choke and sputter.

"It was all his fault," Anna continued her bland explanation. "He wanted to buy my body. Have me 'at his service,' I think his exact words were."

Anna leaned back in her chair and sipped thoughtfully at her tea, as if trying to recall the precise details.

Having the normally unflappable Jane in shock was an opportunity that wasn't likely to come up again any time soon. She wanted to be sure and enjoy every minute of it.

"And I didn't ask him to show me his. I just moaned a lot and said things like, 'yes, more, deeper'," she added. "You know, like that movie you made me watch with you, where the woman fakes an orgasm in a diner," Anna concluded.

Jane's mouth moved wordlessly.

"So how was your night?" Anna went on in bright tones.

As an attempt to deflect the conversation, it failed.

Jane found her voice.

"Anna, you know I'm always telling you to get out and date but are you really sure you've thought this through?" Real worry colored her alto tones.

It was nice to hear, Anna decided. She had quite a support system. Good friends like Jane were few and far between.

Had she ever told Jane how much their friendship meant to her? Anna didn't think so. But she thought her friend's generous nature had nurtured her in a lot of ways and allowed her to grow to the point that she could take off in daring new directions.

Last night's boldness hadn't sprung from nowhere.

It was more the culmination of seeds of esteem planted and sprouted with care.

"Jane, did I ever tell you I love you like a sister?"

Jane blinked in surprise. "You're not getting around me, boss, I'm worried about you."

"I know, and I appreciate it. Who else would worry about me? You're my best friend. You adopted me and shared your family with me." Anna paused and frowned. "I'd share my family with you but even I don't like them. Besides, they live on the other coast."

She sipped some more chamomile meditatively while she struggled for words. She was learning how to communicate better, wasn't she? She could communicate better with Jane, too.

"You really went out of your way to help out and free me up to do creative work. You've made my job a lot easier. And you made a real effort to draw me out."

Jane just stared at her.

"I just did what anyone would do."

"No, you didn't," Anna assured her. "Jay's right, you are nice. And I'm lucky to have you as an assistant and as a friend."

"He said I was nice?" Jane was startled. Then she narrowed her eyes. "No, I'm not falling for it. Give. I want to hear everything. Every word, every detail, from the top."

She started to tap her foot again, a sure sign she was losing patience.

"That's everything. I went dressed to kill, or at least maim, he got out of line while we were dancing—"

"Dancing? You distinctly did not mention dancing before," Jane declared, pouncing on the detail like a tigress.

"So sue me," Anna tossed back, grinning. "We danced. He dances like Fred Astaire, too."

Jane made appropriate swooning noises.

"He got a little carried away, so I stepped on him, which is why he said he was limping. And he was deliberately trying to intimidate me by talking dirty to me. So I did it back. It got to him."

The memory of that stunning victory did a great deal to restore Anna's confidence. He might be bad but she was catching up fast.

Jane rolled her eyes in patent disbelief. "Oh, and you're surprised at this? No wonder he said you liked him. So, do you like him?"

Did she? Anna didn't know. She would have sworn she didn't in spite of the unmistakable attraction she felt toward him but that was before the French kiss experiment that had left her books littering the floor.

She wondered if she should mention her new branch of experimentation to Jane but decided not to. She'd had enough shocks for one day.

She settled for a mild, "I don't know."

"Uh-huh."

"Well, I don't. He's egotistical and rude. He was condescending. He said with a body like mine I'd never be mistaken for a rocket scientist." Indignation sounded in her voice at the memory.

Jane lost it. She doubled over, laughing. "Get out of town! He said that? He really said that? Oh, my God, he must have died. Didn't he know who you were?"

A wry smile quirked Anna's lips. "Evidently not."

Jane laughed again. "So, aside from not being very quick on the uptake, he's a great dancer and obviously a great kisser. Take notes on lunch and let me know how he scores."

"Sure," Anna agreed. "Now, maybe we should do something really revolutionary, like get to work."

"Yes, boss," Jane smirked. "Wouldn't want you to be late leaving for lunch."

They both burst out laughing again.

As Anna gathered up her fallen books, she sobered. Once again, the gap between theory and practice was evident. She'd seen French kisses on the big screen, read descriptive narrative, heard Jane's blow-by-blow accounts of steamy dates. But none of that had prepared her for the awesome sensation of Jay's heated mouth on hers, his tongue curling around hers.

Were all kisses like that? It was really a problem, not having anything to compare it to. Every experiment she'd ever conducted had had a baseline, a control. Something to gauge the results by.

Maybe she should have asked Tom, the limo driver, to kiss her. Aesthetically, the two men were equally attractive. Theoretically, kissing them should be equally enjoyable. Unless there were factors she wasn't taking into consideration.

Well, in spite of her ignorance and inexperience, she hadn't done too badly. Jay had said she was good.

From the way he talked, he should know.

The real question was, to Anna's way of thinking, was he good?

And if he wasn't, how could she tell?

Maybe she'd find some hints in her new books. Meanwhile, she should follow her own advice and get to work.

And she could practice more kissing at lunch. One important key to research was the ability to repeat a test. If the results couldn't be duplicated predictably, they didn't mean anything. Anna figured that if he could kiss her again and cause her to lose track of time, knock over objects unnoticed, raise her body temperature by at least a full degree and speed up her heart rate to an aerobic workout level, she still wouldn't know how good he was at kissing, comparatively, but she'd know that was normal for him, at least.

Anna wondered if she should start a file and document her new line of research. No, maybe not. She was exploring and discovering her own sexuality and she really didn't think something called "Anna Does Anything" should be put to paper.

At least she'd learned that she could do whatever she decided to put her mind to and do it well, including, it seemed, French kissing. Also the fine art of saying decidedly unsweet nothings. And then there was her masterful demonstration of social self-defense on the dance floor.

All in all, she thought she was making speedy progress.

And she'd learned that she didn't have to particularly like a man to like kissing him, which came as a surprise.

Or was she being unfair? She really didn't know Jay Whitman well enough to like or dislike him. He was mouthy and obnoxious but he was also oddly innocent about it. She really didn't think he'd meant to hurt her with any of the things he'd said.

If she was honest with herself, she had to admit that it was hard to dislike someone who admired her for stomping on his foot. In fact, he seemed to just plain admire her, no matter what she did.

Anna paused to consider his good points.

He did dance really, really well.

He didn't seem intimidated by either her brains or her beauty.

She'd liked kissing him.

So, he did have some redeeming features but if she was going to experiment with dating and get some experience, she couldn't have him running around claiming they were an item, either.

She'd set him straight at lunch, Anna decided.

Unfortunately, that turned out to be easier to decide than to do.

Anna mentally added "bullheaded" to his long list of faults.

First of all, he breezed back into her office as if he belonged there and it didn't even seem to occur to him that he could be interrupting anything. He seemed to think his presence overrode any other claims on her attention that anyone might have.

He draped himself over Anna's desk, looking like he'd come to take her away from all her labors, and wasn't she thrilled to see him?

She wasn't, actually. She thought she was on to something and didn't want to be interrupted.

But he was impossible to ignore.

"Hey, hot stuff, are you ready to go?" He eyed her up and down with obvious lust that apparently wasn't thwarted by the bulky lab coat she wore over jeans and a knit shirt.

"Don't call me 'hot stuff'," Anna returned.

"Hey, if the shoe fits..." he winked, the smug knowledge of their shared kisses blatantly open on his face.

Anna felt her face begin to burn and cursed her pale redhead complexion.

"You are the hottest thing I've ever seen. No wonder you have all those signs." He waved at the multitude of warnings posted to declare the presence of highly flammable, combustible materials.

Jay traced the outline of her lips with one lazy finger as he remarked, "Dangerous."

Then, without warning, he replaced his finger with his mouth and planted another hot, hard kiss on her unprepared lips.

While she was still off balance from that, he hauled her to her feet, grabbed her purse and hustled her out the door.

"Come on, passion flower, lunch awaits."

Before she knew it, she found herself stuffed into a soft leather bucket seat and sped away to an unknown destination where, presumably, food could be found.

"Stop calling me all those names. I have a name," she informed him firmly, determined to take control of the situation.

"I know. Anna. Anna, the beautiful." He winked at her again as he rhapsodized over her name.

"Just 'Anna' will do."

"No, I don't think so," Jay mused. "Pet names are a way of showing affection. I feel very affectionate toward you." Heavy innuendo accompanied his breezy declaration and he captured her hand to nibble on her palm.

"I noticed." But the sour tone of her voice evidently bounced off him as he continued to shower her with affection whether she wanted it or not.

"Stop that," she finally snapped and dragged her hand away.

He gave her a disappointed look.

"You don't find hands an erogenous zone? Okay, I'll start with your feet next time."

Anna sighed. "No, you won't."

"No feet either? You're a real challenge. I guess I'll have to start with your back, then. Lots of nerve centers there," Jay stated enthusiastically. "Then I'll work my way around to your—"

"Keep your verbal hands to yourself," Anna muttered. The whole conversation was ridiculous.

"But I can't use my real hands," he pointed out. "I'm driving."

This just wasn't going to work, Anna realized in dismay. No matter what she said, it just sailed directly over his swollen head. The man had to have an ego the size of Texas.

While she fumed internally, they arrived at the restaurant.

There wasn't a wait. They were led promptly to a quiet corner table and seated. Jay proceeded to play footsies with her under the cover provided by the tablecloth.

Anna glared at him.

Jay smiled at her.

"Aren't you concerned about the safety of your feet?" Anna asked in annoyance.

"Nope. You aren't wearing heels." He scanned the lunch menu left by the hostess. "What sounds good to you? Do you like seafood? Salads?"

So he didn't see her as a threat without heels? Anna hauled off and delivered a solid kick to his shin as she replied, "Oh, I have varied tastes."

It was the wrong thing to say. Far from discouraged, he looked intrigued. "I look forward to helping you experiment."

Then again, Anna reflected, it seemed that all paths led to the same destination in his mind. No matter what she said he'd find a sexual meaning in it. No matter how deep he had to dig to do it.

"In food," she clarified.

"I've heard of things you can do with food." He sounded even more interested and ready to try them all.

Anna sighed again and was rescued by the waitress coming to take their order.

The worst thing, she realized, was that his constant references to sex, combined with her sudden interest in the subject and the memory of the exciting discovery of the wonders of French kissing, had her wondering if she should take him up on his offer to help her in her research.

He had offered, of his own free choice. She'd admitted she did need some experience. If he was even half as able as his constant bragging implied, he was certainly well qualified to provide her with some. Although it sounded heartlessly clinical.

Still, the physical and emotional didn't have to go together, did they? And it wasn't as if he was offering her his heart and soul. It was his body he was apparently dying to give her.

And no shabby offer, either, Anna realized. She let her eyes roam over him as thoroughly as he had eyed her. Clothes could hide a lot but she thought he was fairly athletic, judging from his dancing demonstration. He couldn't be too badly out of shape. Also, that he was fully equipped and ready to proceed had been distinctly obvious.

She did remember his happiness at meeting her.

No, he wouldn't have any problem performing.

All in all, he looked like one long, tall specimen of masculinity wrapped in an expensive business suit.

With a very nice tie.

She hadn't noticed before but the silk, patterned in a swirling paisley with blues and greens, did a lot for his rather dramatic monochrome coloring, extended by the neutral gray suit and white shirt.

He was an attractive man, in a chisel-featured, satanic sort of way. And his little-boy charm gave him an added edge of innocence and danger.

He was obnoxious.

He couldn't be trusted.

He'd probably try to find some way to turn her new line of research to his advantage.

But he was, all around, a good candidate for her introduction to the pleasures of the flesh.

Now, how did she determine if he was all talk or if he was genuinely an enthusiastic explorer of any erotic discoveries with a gift in seeking out erogenous zones?

The arrival of lunch gave Anna something else to think about and she thankfully busied herself with her grilled chicken salad.

But when Jay started toying with her feet again, she decided not to kick him.

Chapter Five

"Is that as good as it looks?"

The plaintive question, combined with the wistful eyes fixed on Anna's chicken salad, were a clear hint that Jay wanted to find out the only possible way—by firsthand experience.

Anna could understand that. She'd been increasingly interested in expanding her firsthand experiences, too.

And she doubted that the question was prompted by dissatisfaction with his own lunch. The corned beef sandwich on rye bread looked tempting enough. So did the crisp french fries.

No, from the way his foot was insinuating itself between both of hers, there was only one thing on his lecherous mind and it wasn't salad.

He wanted her to feed him a bite.

This was probably one of those things he'd heard about doing with food and wanted to try. It sounded a lot less messy and far safer than something she'd heard about doing with whipped cream. So Anna forked up a bite of succulent chicken and offered it to him.

His eyes gleamed in approval and he took the bite slowly off her fork, taking time to enjoy the full flavor.

"Not bad," he said finally. "Not as good as your hand, but not bad."

He would remind her about his affectionate hand-kissing. Obnoxious man. Still, Anna thought she was coming to appreciate his potential usefulness. There was also the fact that when his lips were busy kissing, they were blessedly silent. Something worth considering seriously.

"It's going to cost you a french fry," Anna declared. She thought it was time for her to push back a little. She'd enjoyed feeding him. It wasn't the heady, overwhelming sensation produced by his skillful kissing, but still a pleasant sensation nonetheless. Being fed by him just might be enjoyable, too.

Jay selected a fry for her and fed it to her. One finger brushed a trace of salt from the corner of her mouth when she finished.

"Like it?"

The smoldering heat in the ebony depths of his eyes told her exactly what he was asking.

"Mmm. I'm not sure. Maybe you should try another one," Anna suggested finally, as if making up her mind.

He offered her another salty fry and she couldn't resist pushing him a little further. She parted her lips just enough to admit the fry and slid her mouth down over it almost to the point that his fingers held it at. Then she slid back up a teasing bit before biting it off.

Jay retaliated by slipping a foot free of one shoe and running it from between her ankles up to push her knees apart.

Startled, Anna tightened her knees to keep him from going any further.

Above the table, he reached for her hands with both of his and captured them in a warm hold. She looked from his hands to his face and found herself caught by the intensity of his gaze.

"Don't be afraid of me."

The earnest tone was a surprise to her. Almost as much of a surprise as his suddenly serious expression.

"I'm not afraid," Anna replied. "I'm not sure about this. I think you're going too fast."

Jay didn't think he was going nearly fast enough. She had to know what she was doing to him. She'd tied him up in sweet knots with her first look across a crowded room. She'd stood close enough to burn him with her heat and verbally sparred with him in a spicy exchange that only made him hungry for more.

After she'd bitten his earlobe and moaned, "More. Deeper. I want you now, Jay," she could tell him he was going too fast? He didn't think so.

And then there was that kiss.

He burned just thinking about it, her honeyed lips and the incredible womanly softness even a lab coat couldn't hide. He'd felt it against him when she danced with him and he'd felt it under him when he kissed her on her desk.

It wasn't enough. He ached to touch her. He held her still with his firm grip on her hands and moved his foot sensuously against her knees.

"Nobody can see," he said with warm persuasion. "We're just another business couple having lunch. Nothing unusual about that. We're perfectly ordinary. Except for your lab coat, that does kind of stick out." The teasing note at the end failed to coax a smile from her.

Jay kept slowly stroking her legs with his foot. "Come on, beautiful. Relax. I'm only going to touch you with my toes."

Anna met his eyes steadily while she considered his suggestion. He was right, nobody could see anything under their table. Even if the room had been crowded, they were at the wrong angle in their corner for visibility. Added to that, the draping tablecloths would have hidden a lot more than a game of footsies.

The real question was, did she want him to go any further?

She wasn't sure. The light patterns his foot drew on her thighs felt good. Warm and pleasurable. She could carry the test a little further and see if she continued to enjoy it. If she didn't, she could stop him at any time, heels or no heels.

Anna made a decision and parted her knees to let his wayward foot slide further.

He didn't rush. He made his slow, steady way to the junction of her thighs and nestled there, very gently but firmly. He settled his foot snugly against her.

It felt warm, Anna decided. Warm and welcome. The gentle pressure he created as he slowly shifted the length of his foot against her gradually recreated the same tingling sensation his velvet tongue sliding over and around hers had. And the same heated hunger for more.

When he slowly withdrew his foot, she immediately missed the pressure and the warmth.

Jay smiled at her. "I think I found an erogenous zone you like."

"You think so?"

"Oh, yes. But I really think you ought to keep an open mind about hands and feet," he answered solemnly. Then he gestured at her to eat but kept one of her hands trapped in his while they continued with the meal.

As if to prove his point, he traced circles and lines all over the sensitive surface of her palm, fingers and wrist, which produced the same phenomena of raised body temperature, increased heart rate and loss of time-sense as his hot, deep kisses.

Anna concluded that the mouthy playboy wasn't all talk. He was, in fact, an expert. He probably knew erogenous zones and erotic techniques, what a g-spot was and how to find hers.

He was a gold mine of knowledge and practical experience of the very hands-on variety and if anyone could bring her up to speed, he could.

Anna polished off her salad in a fog of sensual anticipation.

She wanted to make up for lost time. Lost play. Lost experiences. She wanted to try everything and do the fun things twice. She didn't want to grow old regretting all the chances never taken, all the hours not fully lived.

She didn't want to look back at this moment and wonder what would have happened next, if only.

If only she'd dared. If only she'd boldly asked for what she wanted.

And right now, she wanted to find out what would happen if he played with every inch of her body the way he was playing with her hand.

She wanted to know what else they could try with food.

She wanted to know what it would feel like if he kept teasing her with his toes.

She wanted to know if she could do the same to him and if he'd like it.

She wanted him.

So this was what desire felt like, Anna acknowledged silently. Maybe she was getting a late start but better late than never. She'd always been a good student and a quick study. She'd pick it up. Starting right now.

Anna drank some ice water to wash down the last of her salad, took a deep breath and asked, "Have you had a blood test and do you have a copy of your sexual history?"

She regretted the directness of her question when he nearly choked to death on a french fry. She jumped up to pound him on his back in a helpful gesture. Then she pushed his glass of water into his hand.

"Here, drink this. It'll help," she suggested.

He continued to cough weakly but he waved her back to her seat. After he took several deep breaths, he picked up the glass, drank the water and then managed to gasp out, "Honey, you do know how to get right to the point."

Had she acted prematurely? Anna didn't think so. He'd had his foot between her legs. He'd French kissed her on her desk. He'd propositioned her the night before and she didn't think he'd invited her to his place to impress her with his interior decorating skills.

But, she decided, it couldn't hurt to be clear.

"Was that too soon to ask? I thought you wanted to have sex with me."

Jay started to cough and choke again.

Anna waited for him to regain his composure. She didn't jump up to pound between his shoulder blades this time, since she didn't think he was in any danger of inhaling a bite of food.

Still, it made her nervous until he recovered.

"Honey. Oh, honey. Do I want to have sex with you?" He looked dazed. "I want to put you into orbit. I want to make you scream."

Screaming? In enjoyment, she hoped. Or maybe there was a whole lot more to this than she'd thought. Anna remembered a little shop in Hollywood that carried a full line of bondage accessories and clothing. Maybe he was into spanking. Although, what did she know? Maybe spanking was fun. If it wasn't, she didn't know why it had ever managed to become popular with any segment of the population.

She decided not to worry about his preferences for now. She had other details to think about.

"Good. So what about the blood test?" Anna asked in what she hoped was a firm but polite tone.

It was a sticky point. She didn't want to harp on it but she did have a responsibility to think this through, after all. Even she knew safe sex was a priority.

Jay cleared his throat with some difficulty. "Ah, I, um. I had one, fairly recently. Ah, since I was pretty active. I wasn't in a high risk group or anything," he hastened to assure her. "I practiced safe sex anyway but I wanted to be sure. I don't have anything."

To Anna's amazement, he actually seemed embarrassed.

Incredible.

The man with all the demonstrable sensitivity of a rhinoceros, embarrassed? It hadn't bothered him at all to offer to buy the use of her body. It hadn't bothered him to make blatantly sexual overtures on the dance floor and in her office. He hadn't been the slightest bothered by either her kicking him under the table or his little sexy games.

So why did one little question that was an unfortunate fact of life bother him?

She hoped he wasn't hiding something. "And since then you've continued to practice safe sex?" she prompted. She had to be sure. It was her body. She wanted to fully enjoy life, not subject herself to any life-threatening diseases.

To her further disbelief, Anna saw that he was now actually blushing.

"I've been, uh, ah," he mumbled. He seemed unable to focus.

A horrifying thought struck her.

Maybe he was into worse things than spanking.

"You've been what?" she demanded sharply.

Expert or not, some things weren't worth risking. It would be too bad if she couldn't have the first man she'd ever truly desired but she'd find another one.

Jay cleared his throat again. "I changed my, ah, habits a while ago, okay? Things are different now. Even if you're careful the only way to be sure is to get tested. The whole testing thing made me rethink some of my priorities. You might say I've had one partner—" he stopped again and swore under his breath.

He was so completely discomfited, he could only mean one thing.

He really was a lover of self.

Anna couldn't help it. She started to laugh.

She figured that was a mistake when he practically threw money on their table, grabbed her arm and rushed her outside to start up his car but it was so funny.

All this time, she'd been so worried about her lack of experience. And the great playboy himself had been practicing celibacy with a vengeance.

Anna wondered ridiculously just what he'd had in mind for them when he'd propositioned her. Side-by-side twin beds, while they exchanged ever-hotter naughty words?

At that thought, she laughed even harder. Soon tears rolled down her cheeks. She was so lost in the irony of it all that she didn't pay any attention to where they were going until the car stopped and he shut the engine off.

It took a few minutes to register that they weren't back in the office parking lot. Instead, they were parked outside of a shuttered cape house.

This must be where he lived, she realized slowly. Then he was ushering her inside and pushing her down to sit on a comfortable plush sofa.

While she watched, he paced around in silence for a few minutes before he started to talk.

"Listen, this is pretty awkward to talk about but you're right, you're entitled to ask. Up until I decided to have the test, I didn't take it very seriously. It was all just fun and games." He paused and turned to face her.

"I was always careful because I feel very strongly about being responsible. I mean, I believe children shouldn't be unwanted accidents."

Anna nodded, matching his seriousness. It seemed expected of her. In fact, this was eerily like sitting through one of Lyle's lectures. She supposed she could be thankful that Jay didn't wave cigars and bang his fists for emphasis.

She supposed the least she could do in thankfulness for being spared those extremes was to listen politely.

He continued earnestly, "Then I realized even that wasn't enough. I didn't just want to play games. I wanted it to mean something."

He paused again to gather his thoughts.

"I knew that so far I didn't have any permanent consequences. I didn't want to risk changing that in pursuit of fun. I knew I wanted to get married and have children one day."

Anna tried to look like she understood where he was going with that and threw in another sober nod since it seemed appropriate.

He walked over to join her on the sofa and took her hands in his as he finished, "So there hasn't been anybody since. Okay? That's pretty safe."

Safe? Anna couldn't help feeling a bit skeptical. "If that's true, then why have you been heading straight for the nearest bedroom since the minute we met?"

Jay looked uncomfortable again and sighed. "I was afraid you'd ask something like that. Tell me, do rocket scientists believe in love at first sight?"

"I don't have enough information to believe or not believe," Anna answered.

He persisted, "Well, will you accept it as a working theory, anyway?"

She didn't see any harm in that. "Okay," she agreed cautiously.

"Okay." Jay was silent for a minute. Then he said something that she guessed, in retrospect, she probably should have seen coming. "I love you."

"Oh," was all she could think of to say to that.

It was too bad. No, it was worse than that. She was crushingly disappointed. She'd wanted to play with him and now he was as far off-limits as he would have been if he'd had a fatal disease.

It wouldn't be fair to use him when she didn't return his feelings, Anna concluded glumly.

"'Oh'? Is that all you have to say, 'oh'? Listen, I didn't want to bring this up but you asked." Jay sounded distinctly huffy.

"Oh," Anna repeated stupidly. "Well, thank you for being so up-front with me about your history. I'm sorry we can't have sex now. Shall we get back to work?" she finished brightly.

"No, we aren't going back to work now. If you're worried about it, we have orders to bury the hatchet. But I think you should forget about work for once. You work practically every night and weekend as it is. You could take a month off and Lyle would probably cheer. And I've been putting in a lot of overtime myself setting up the new marketing plan. You wanted to talk. You started this and now we're not going anywhere until we finish it." Jay concluded his speech on a rather forceful note.

He pushed on, "We are going to be lovers, so now why don't you reciprocate and tell me about your history?"

Anna looked at him. Having become forbidden fruit, he suddenly looked even better. Unfair that he had to go and make himself unattainable when he was within grasp. Then she pushed down the regrets. She didn't have time for them.

"I'm afraid we aren't going to become lovers, so—"

"The hell we aren't." He went from forceful to loud indignation.

"No. We aren't." Anna repeated herself clearly and firmly in case there was any possible misunderstanding.

"Yes, we are," he snapped and pushed her down on the couch before he sprawled full-length on top of her.

"We are not." Anna glowered at him, unwilling to let the situation deteriorate further and turn into a wrestling match. She clung to reason instead and held still.

Unfortunately, Jay didn't seem terribly interested in reason at the moment.

"Are too." His volume increased significantly.

"We are not." She matched him for loudness.

"Are too," he practically yelled.

"Get off of me," she shouted back.

"No. You wanted to have sex, didn't you? Me, too. I think we should just move right ahead, just as soon as you answer me."

He was back to being arrogant, obnoxious, pigheaded, insufferable... Anna ran out of descriptions.

"Get off of me. You're too heavy," she gritted out between clenched teeth.

"No, I'm not," Jay assured her, suddenly back to seductive sexual confidence. He moved against her to demonstrate. "That feels good, doesn't it? You're as tall as I am. My weight isn't too much for you."

His legs slid hers apart and he pushed her deeper into the sofa cushions.

He was right. His weight did feel good. Comfortably heavy and solid. Excitingly strong. His slow rocking movements were building pleasurable tingles everywhere.

Jay's mouth closed over hers again, probably because he'd realized the conversation was going nowhere fast.

Anna wished faintly that she could see a clock to keep track of whether or not she lost all sense of time again.

Then she forgot about it as he coaxed her lips apart and slid his tongue inside to curl with hers, building a hungry heat in the cradle of her pelvis that radiated to a sharp, throbbing point between her legs.

She might as well enjoy his kissing, she decided. Anna opened her mouth further and kissed him back, thrusting her own tongue into his mouth.

Jay made a hoarse sound of encouragement and deepened the kiss, matching the swirling, teasing motions of his tongue with the movement of his body on hers.

Hot, wet, wild and deep, his kisses had her moving underneath him in an effort to get closer.

"You like that, don't you, passion flower?" he murmured against her ear before he licked it.

Anna shivered at the unfamiliar sensation and nodded silently.

He nibbled his way down the curve of her neck. "And that. You like that, too, don't you, sweetheart?"

"Yes," she whispered faintly and arched against his solid weight.

"And this?" He nipped lightly at the curve of one full breast and she gasped. "I guess that means yes." His voice held pure male satisfaction.

Jay rolled her out of her lab coat and hauled her long-sleeved knit shirt over her head. Then Anna found out what those little lines and circles drawn with his fingers felt like all over her bared torso.

Torture.

It wasn't enough. She wanted more of him. More direct pressure in some places. More of his kisses. More of his tongue. More of his heavy body rocking on hers. Frustrated, she moved under his hands, trying to direct them to the twin peaks that ached for his touch.

He complied, closing his hands over her breasts and cupping their full weight easily. She sighed in pleasure at the new sensation of his hands holding her breasts, stroking and rubbing lazy circles around the sensitized nipples.

"Good, isn't it?" Jay asked as he licked the valley in between.

"Yes."

He pulled her bra straps down and reached behind her to unfasten it. Then he freed her from the restricting garment. Cold air hit her naked breasts before his warm hands closed back over them, skin to heated skin.

"And that's even better, isn't it, honey?" He didn't wait for a reply but moved his hot mouth down over her full curves while his thumbs rubbed her nipples until she cried out softly.

It was a whole lot better.

"You like it all, my hands, my kisses, my body on yours, don't you?" His voice was thick with passion.

"Yes," Anna gasped.

Jay knelt over her, one knee planted firmly between her spread legs, and lifted her rib cage as he closed his lips over one nipple. He sucked gently, drawing more of her into his mouth with devastating results. Her head dropped back, the resulting arch offering her curves more fully up to his attention. He deliberately rode his knee between her thighs until she moved her hips in answer. The pressure that created against her feminine mound, combined with the way his mouth tugged at her breast, would have made her eyes roll back in her head if they'd been open. She was clearly in the hands of a genius.

"Oh, precious, you love that, I know you do," he rasped against her skin before closing over her other breast and tasting more of her. He swirled his tongue around the hardened nub and nipped at it.

Anna sobbed faintly, lost to everything but the incredible pleasure his knowing hands and mouth gave her. She moved restlessly against his thigh and arched closer to him. There was that throbbing point between her legs that wasn't getting enough pressure, enough consistent stimulation.

"You want my weight on you now, sweet?" As he asked, he lifted her higher to lick at her navel. He unsnapped her jeans and peeled her out of them, laying her back down and covering her with himself. "Like that?"

Beyond speech, Anna nodded and wrapped her arms and legs around him in a full-body hug. Without the barrier of her jeans, she could feel the length of his penis right where it felt best, providing increased pressure right where she wanted it. The weight of his body made his penis press deeper into the folds that were growing wet and slick to welcome him. But not deep enough. It occurred to her that it would feel a lot better if he got rid of his pants, too. And her underwear had to go. There were still far too many clothes in the way.

"Hang on tight, honey." Jay stood, using his knee as a lever to raise up from the couch and then straightening his legs to bring them both upright, the differences in their bone structure and musculature apparent in his unexpected strength. He carried her to his bedroom and laid her down. Then he stripped off his jacket and tie, kicked off his shoes, discarded his shirt and wrapped the silk tie around Anna's wrists.

"What—" she began but then he took off the rest of his clothes and her attention was diverted.

He was long and muscular. He had the lean body of a runner or bicyclist as opposed to the bulk of a weight lifter. He was as athletic as she'd guessed.

And he was huge. Was a penis like that normal? Shouldn't it be sort of smaller? She'd read that the average size was six inches, which sounded large but not unmanageable. Clearly some men were running around skewing the curve.

It was never going to work, she realized in sudden panic. She knew physics. She knew her own body. He was too big.

Jay knotted the tie, raised her arms over her head and tied them to the headboard.

"Wait a minute," she protested. "I don't know about this. And I said we weren't going to be lovers. I know I said that. I think you should stop right now."

In answer, he lowered himself over her again and kissed her deeply.

"Are you sure? You might like it. You might try to keep an open mind," he suggested warmly.

"But I don't think—"

"Good," he cut in. "You probably think way too much, way too often. Take a break."

His mouth closed over her curves again, tasting everything from her neck to her waist, nibbling, biting and sucking. He moved lower and pulled off her panties before he continued downward, demonstrating that legs and feet were also erogenous zones.

He nibbled his leisurely way from her ankle to hip and pushed her legs apart. Anna stiffened and he hushed her.

"I want to see you. I want to look at all of you. Let me."

She let him part her legs and he looked down at her red-gold curls.

"You're beautiful," he told her. His hand closed over her mound and cupped her moist heat. His fingers wound through the soft pubic hair and stroked over a sensitive point that nearly levitated her in reaction. "You like that too, don't you?"

Anna nodded slowly.

A tender smile curved his lips at her response.

"You're all soft and warm everywhere. You taste like you sound, like warm honey."

He stroked her as he talked, his hand sliding over and over her mound, the tips of his fingers dipping inside her slick folds to open her slightly, pressing lightly against the sensitized bud of her clitoris. "I love how you look, naked and ready for me."

The more he touched her, the more ready she felt. Amazing what that hand of his could do. She was getting wetter by the second, drenching his fingertips. He slid one finger further inside her and nature's lubrication eased the way. A second finger followed, stretching her, opening her. He slid his thumb over her clitoris again while his fingers penetrated her and it was a good thing she was laying down because her entire body was a boneless pool of need. She needed him naked and close. She needed him to touch her. Most of all, she needed him to keep on doing *that*.

He took his hand away but before she could complain about it he covered her body fully with his again, sliding his legs between hers. His hard, hot member pressed against her slick, swollen flesh, replacing his hand. And that felt even better. Yes, that was exactly where she wanted him, with no clothing to prevent the tip of his penis from sliding between her wet folds. Much, much better with nothing in the way. "Ah. Birth control. Anna, are you on the pill?"

Good question. She exerted herself to come up with a coherent answer. "No. I stopped at my doctor's office for a contraceptive shot this morning. The timing was right. It's good for three months."

He grinned down at her. "So you met me and suddenly decided you needed three months of continuous, fool-proof birth control? That's a good sign."

"I was motivated. Jay, wait, I don't think this is a good idea," she gasped weakly.

He sighed. "Will you forget about the history and the rest? I don't think a woman who works the kind of hours you do has time to go out and practice unsafe sex," he told her impatiently.

"But, Jay—"

He placed his hand over her mouth.

"Hush." Then he replaced his hand with his lips and slid his tongue between hers as he thrust his penis slowly into her body.

Anna jerked against him in shock at the unfamiliar sensation. He was so hot there and she was so wet and he was easing himself in gently but relentlessly while she softened and stretched to make way for him. The contact was incredible but it was the unknown sensation of fullness that undid her. She'd felt so sharply empty without his fingers inside her and now she was being filled to capacity and beyond. And inexplicably she wanted more. She needed him to fill her and fill her with himself and she needed it right now.

"Relax, honey, relax," he soothed, as she moved her hips restlessly to open herself more deeply to him. He kissed her cheek. "You're just tight. It's been a long time for you, too, hasn't it? It's all right, honey, we'll take it slow."

Suiting action to words, he held still until she relaxed slightly, then surged forward, going deeper.

"Jay—"

"Oh, sweetheart, you're tight," he groaned. He buried his face in her hair and held her close. Then he withdrew before abruptly thrusting all the way in, breaking through an unmistakable barrier in the process.

She cried out.

He froze.

"Anna?"

She didn't answer. She couldn't. There were no words in this place, only kaleidoscopic displays of light and color and the amazing fullness between her legs and deep inside where she ached and throbbed. Jay was there with her, inside her, part of her and she wasn't empty anymore.

Jay wrapped his arms even tighter around her. He held her as closely as he could, rocking her in his arms. "Anna. Anna, honey, use your legs and hang on to me."

She did, burying her face in his neck and wrapping her long legs around his waist. That drove him even deeper and she reveled in the sensation.

"That's it," he encouraged. He brushed a soft kiss onto her shoulder. "Just hang on tight."

He withdrew and returned again and again, rocking into her a little more deeply each time.

The initial shock faded and to Anna's disbelief, the laws of physics were overridden, because somehow her body made room for him and even welcomed him.

He was all the way inside her and it felt even better than French kissing. It felt better than anything. Anna could see the benefit of his experience. If he didn't care if she used his body, why should she? She followed his instructions and clung to him as he took more and more of her.

"That's it, honey, open wider," he whispered when he felt her move against him.

She complied and opened her thighs more fully. He surged deeper. She sobbed softly at the sensation and he seemed to sense what she wanted. He ground his hips against hers in a circle as he stayed deeply buried.

His mouth started moving over her breasts again. He suckled gently while grinding his hips against hers and he got his wish.

She screamed. Waves of pleasure shattered her. She pulsed with it and that wrapped her flesh even more tightly around his penis, deep inside her, adding to the sensation and building more pulsing ripples. It seemed endless.

Jay laughed softly in triumph. His chest dragged against her sensitized nipples as he thrust into her in short strokes, then long, deep strokes and then withdrew to plunge fully inside her again. She was wild beneath him, fighting his weight and bucking against his hips to take more of the pleasure he offered.

He took her mouth again. His tongue curled around hers as he possessed her fully and her scream was lost in his kiss as waves of pleasure threatened to rip her apart. Through it he kept pace, pushing her higher, taking her farther and spinning out each climax before pushing her into the next one. Finally, he joined her, pouring his liquid orgasm into her with a deep pulsing that pushed her over the peak of ecstasy and made her scream again.

She didn't know she bit him.

Chapter Six

While Anna lay stunned, Jay reached up to free her and then scooped her up to cradle her on his lap as he leaned against the headboard. He rocked her gently in his arms and stroked the long hair that had spilled loose from her braid.

She clung to him and let him hold her, too deeply shaken to do anything else. She felt ridiculously close to tears.

She hadn't been prepared for the feelings. Not at all. She was shaken by the intensity of her desire, the sharpness of her need and the unspeakable pleasure he'd given her. She didn't have to be a woman of experience to know that Jay was not only a genius in bed, he was also considerate and generous.

He'd made sure she was physically ready for him and then he'd made sure she orgasmed, not just one time but repeatedly, before he did. That was a really good thing, considering the insane level of need she'd reached by the time he got all the way inside her. One orgasm probably wouldn't have been enough to relieve her. In fact, the first one had just sort of paved the way for the rest and it was the final one that he'd shared with her that had left her feeling satisfied and spent and pleasured within an inch of her life. The ability to think was coming back, but slowly. Talking would be a real strain. She'd probably just make incoherent moaning noises in an effort to express her gratitude for the multiple orgasms and the size of his penis, which had turned out to be just perfect for her.

She sincerely, fervently and deeply hoped he didn't want to talk just then.

"Honey," he whispered against her cheek. "Oh, honey. You should have told me. I didn't want to hurt you."

Anna could hear the sincere regret in his voice and thought she should probably say something reassuring but she'd only been practicing improved communication for two days and this situation was beyond her. If she managed to say anything, it was bound to be something hopelessly unsophisticated. For instance, it was probably considered tacky to thank him for having the foresight to tie her up before pounding her into the mattress. That had definitely added something to the experience. Amazons didn't get many opportunities to feel feminine and helpless. "Oh, honey," he said again softly. Jay hugged her closer as if she was small and fragile and precious.

It was a new feeling. A nice one. This must be what it felt like to be cherished, she decided.

Maybe it wasn't so bad if he loved her.

Anna curled into him and soaked up his warmth and love and comfort. She needed it. Fortunately, his expertise extended to cuddling afterwards. She wouldn't have even known enough to ask for it. Cuddling was definitely good.

While he cuddled her, he stroked her with gentle hands. "My love. My sweet love, you're so beautiful." His voice was soft with emotion.

Compliments were good, too. Anna was suddenly very glad he also gave compliments. She hadn't realized it but she was really feeling the need for some reassurance.

Why hadn't she guessed it would be such a frightening, powerful experience? She'd never felt anything that strongly. It was as if all the pent-up emotions of years had come rushing out when he touched her. She wasn't just spent physically, she was spent emotionally. She felt wrung out and exhausted and her whole body felt limp and heavy as if she'd just woken from a deep sleep.

A gentle rain of kisses covered her bright hair and his hands explored all of her as he rocked her on his lap. When his hand brushed against her feminine mound, she jerked away, overly sensitive to the touch.

"Sore?"

She nodded silently.

Jay scooped her up and carried her though to the master bathroom and turned on the shower. When it heated up, he stood with her under the spray. His body held her up and his arms steadied her when he set her on her feet.

That was good, too, she thought blissfully. Anna wrapped her arms around his waist and leaned her weight against him. It was nice to be held and carried like a child. Nice to have his solid support until her legs were working right again. She knew he wouldn't let her fall. She thought she could almost feel his strength seeping into her bones through the close contact.

After a while, Jay soaped her from head to toe in unhurried strokes then rinsed her with welcome hot water. Then he pulled her close again and simply held her until the hot water gave out.

He had big, thick towels, Anna noted in approval when he helped her out of the shower and wrapped her in one. He pulled one around his own waist then picked up two more and a brush. With his free hand, he took hers and led her back to bed.

Jay sat against the headboard, slung a towel around his neck to absorb the excess moisture and spread his legs to make a place for her to sit. A tug on her hand brought her down and Anna willingly sat in the cradle of his thighs.

He brushed her hair in long, leisurely strokes then wrapped another towel around her shoulders to dry the flame-colored cascade.

That done, he settled her back against his chest and wrapped his arms around her waist. His crossed hands cupped her breasts over the thick terrycloth.

Anna rested quietly with him. She didn't remember ever feeling so warm and cared for. His possessive hold felt like a sweet affirmation of the pleasure they'd shared. From her vantage point, she could see most of his bedroom. She was glad to see the personal touches that gave it life and color.

She was learning more about him. For instance, she now knew that he liked white towels. The bathroom was all white and green. She wasn't sure but she thought she remembered wall-to-wall carpeting throughout his house. In here it was white. Cherry furniture with more green in the quilt that covered the bed and the valances above his windows in a paisley pattern.

That stirred an unsettling thought.

"I hope I didn't ruin your quilt."

Jay groaned. "You don't say anything, until I think maybe I killed or at least ruptured you, and then you worry about a quilt? Forget about the quilt. I can't believe you would worry about something like that at a time like this."

He turned and tugged her down to lay beside him. He unwrapped her from the towel and ran his hands over her again.

"Does it hurt? Are you all right?" The concern in his voice told her again that he cared deeply.

"It hurts a little. Like a muscle ache."

He brushed her legs apart and touched her gently. "Let me see."

She did, holding still for his careful exploration.

"It looks like everything's okay," he said finally.

Satisfied that she was undamaged physically, he pulled her back into his embrace and rubbed her back.

"Oh, honey, you really surprised me," he informed her. "I'm glad you waited. I didn't expect it. But I'm glad." He lifted her chin and stroked her cheek. "I don't want you to think I didn't like being first. I was just surprised, that's all." Black eyes showed concern as they looked into hers. "I was unprepared. I didn't handle it as well as I could have. Okay?"

Anna gave a slight nod of understanding, although she was as far from understanding whatever he was saying as it was probably possible to get. Was the crazy man apologizing for not making it better? If so, it seemed there was a whole lot more to this than she'd ever suspected. She'd barely survived the onslaught of pleasure he'd unleashed. Better would probably have killed her, although she would certainly have died happy.

At her nod he seemed relieved. He gave her a smile and hugged her tight again. "Oh, honey. I can't tell you how glad I am that you've never loved anybody else."

After that intensely passionate declaration, Jay was quiet for a few minutes. Then he couldn't seem to resist teasing her. "I guess you don't have to tell me your history."

"I guess not," Anna mumbled against his chest.

"Told you we were going to be lovers."

His voice was unbearably smug, she thought, but she was too comfortable to jab him in the ribs. Instead, she gave him a verbal jab.

"We aren't lovers just because we had sex once."

"Oh. Right. We're lovers because you lusted after my body."

She did jab his ribs then. "Stop saying that. We aren't lovers." Something about that label made her deeply nervous.

"Don't be even more ridiculous," Jay told her. "We are absolutely, unquestionably lovers now. I realize you may not know this, being inexperienced, but trust me on this one. We are lovers."

"Are not," Anna muttered.

"Are too." He rolled and brought her under him before he kissed her again, long, deep, wet and sweet. "This is mine," he informed her possessively, touching her mouth. "And this." His mouth closed over her breasts in turn. "And this is mine." He kissed her flat belly and hips. "And this, this is definitely, most certainly mine." He kissed her deflowered curls.

It felt soothing. Anna sighed happily.

"That feels good?"

She nodded.

Jay kissed her again with gentle care, his mouth traveling the length of her nether lips in lazy exploration. The kisses gradually grew longer and more varied, suckling at her here, sliding over her there. Then he licked his way inside her. She shuddered. He flicked his tongue over her clitoris and she moaned. His mouth closed around that incredibly sensitive bud and his tongue flicked at it over and over while he suckled her most intimate flesh. The combination probably destroyed brain tissue but she didn't want it to end. She thrust her hips up frantically and he took the hint, using his tongue to thrust inside her in long, slow strokes until she shuddered in orgasm from the ministrations of his mouth.

"Face it, we are lovers," he stated firmly as he moved back up to meet her eye to eye.

Anna thought about it.

"Okay, what if we are?" She gave him a challenging look.

He grinned at her, looking so full of himself that it was positively revolting to see. Except that she thought that he just might have reason to feel that way.

He really was one great lover.

"Why, honey, I'm surprised you have to ask." Wicked enjoyment sparkled in his ebony eyes as he settled himself between her legs again. That he was ready for more was evident even to a beginner. His penis was hard and thick and pearled with moisture at the tip. She was slick and ready from his mouth and the extra moisture made him slide easily into position. The head of his penis slipped inside her and her flesh opened for him and closed around him without resistance. He lowered himself onto her and thrust all the way into her simultaneously.

"Jay, I don't think—" she began but he cut her off with a kiss. It was almost as bad as a lecture from Lyle for getting a chance to speak, she thought irritably.

"I'm glad to hear it, love," he whispered against her mouth. "Don't think. Just feel."

His husky advice was followed swiftly by her second demonstration of his amazing prowess.

It was much slower this time. He was gentle with her, controlled and tender, but no less passionate. She knew another man might have forgotten himself and injured her, but Jay was unexpectedly sensitive.

Maybe, Anna thought, surrendering to his sweet loving, his brash, bold, bad exterior was all a bluff to hide a heart of soft, malleable gold.

Certainly it hid a clever and caring lover.

So they were lovers, she decided. So what? She'd made a good choice in spite of her ignorance. She really was a genius.

Anna kissed him back thoroughly and proceeded to moan lustily in his ear with all the naughty phrases he'd seemed to so enjoy on their first meeting.

It was just as effective in a horizontal position as it had been in a vertical position, she noted with gleeful scientific precision.

"Yes, Jay," she sighed happily. "Oh, yes. Deeper. Oh, Jay."

His response delighted her. She wasn't the only one getting a sensory overload. His whole body shuddered with the effort of restraint as he thrust deeply into her, sliding in and out in a steady rhythm that allowed her time to adjust to his size with each long stroke, pausing each time he buried himself fully inside for her to squirm against the length of him and revel in the sensation of being deeply penetrated.

Then she proceeded to show him just what kind of fireworks she was capable of creating in any situation, with any materials at hand.

He seemed suitably impressed.

Afterwards, content and secure, she slept like a child in his arms.

Much, much too soon, she felt herself being shaken gently.

"Anna. Anna, wake up. Wake up, love." The low whisper was punctuated by little kisses that covered her eyes, nose and cheeks.

She batted at him ineffectually with one hand.

"Wake up, baby, wake up," he crooned.

"No."

"Yes."

"Don't want to."

The bed moved as he got up and Anna curled deeper into the quilt. Good. Now she could go back to sleep.

The quilt was unceremoniously hauled back and Anna made a sleepy protest that went ignored.

"Come on! Get dressed," Jay said. Then he thrust her discarded clothes into her hands.

"No." She stubbornly refused to open her eyes. "It's the middle of the night, Jay."

"Yes! Right!" he enthused. Then he proceeded to demonstrate that he was equally talented at stuffing her back into her clothes as he was at peeling her out of them.

"Maybe you didn't hear me," Anna groaned. She made another try for clearer communication. "The middle of the night. It's the middle of the night, you madman."

"I know! That's the best time," he informed her with truly despicable cheerfulness.

"For what, besides sleeping?" Anna demanded, opening one eye.

"For going where all roads in Maine lead." He hauled her limp form up to stand her on her feet and eyed her critically. "Sweetheart, you look beautiful but your hair's kind of a mess."

Jay turned to rummage in a closet briefly. He came back with a baseball cap in his hands and stuck it on her head. Working quickly, he twisted her long hair and pulled it through the gap in the back to make a makeshift ponytail. Then a few quick strokes with the brush smoothed the length.

"There," he decided, satisfied that she was ready. "You look adorable." The grinning madman kissed the tip of her nose, took her by the hand and pulled her toward the door.

"Jay, what are you doing?" Anna protested as she followed him with dragging steps.

Then it struck her. Maybe this was lover etiquette, taking her home in the middle of the night. Maybe she snored. Maybe he didn't like to share his pillows.

Well, if so, she didn't think much of lover etiquette. If he didn't want to sleep with her, why couldn't he leave instead of rudely waking her up? She opened her mouth to tell him what she thought about his manners.

But he answered her question before she could speak.

"Honey, I told you already. Weren't you listening?" He turned back to look at her and asked, "Where do all roads in Maine lead?"

Anna thought hard but it was the middle of the night and cartography wasn't exactly her strong point. "Massachusetts?"

Jay stared at her, dumbfounded. "Hello?" He waved one hand in front of her eyes as if testing for consciousness. "Anyone in there? Sweetheart, you don't get out much, do you?"

She didn't know what to say to that, so she didn't say anything.

Jay hooted. "I don't believe it! You don't know! You've lived here for three years and you really don't know."

The madman was getting back at her for laughing inappropriately at him earlier, she decided.

Two minutes later, Anna decided enough was enough. It wasn't polite to laugh so long at her expense at such a sensitive time in her life. She kicked his shin again.

"Ow!" he yelped and gave her a wounded look. "Okay, okay. Pay attention." He placed his hands on her shoulders, turned her to face him and eyed her seriously. "All roads in Maine lead to L.L. Bean."

Anna moved her lips soundlessly, repeating the words, but no revelation struck her. What did a store have to do with anything? Maybe lack of sleep had made him unbalanced. Or too much sexual activity after too long a period of abstinence had shorted out his brain.

She said again, "Jay, it's the middle of the night."

He smiled broadly. "Right! That's the best time. During the day, the place is full of tourists." He continued to beam at her, as if he expected her to catch his enthusiasm any minute.

Anna stared blankly back, unable to put the facts together.

"Baby. Sweetheart. You're a woman, right? Women like to go shopping, right?" Looking solemn, he prompted her patiently.

Anna considered that. She'd liked shopping for her new dress. "Yes."

"So I am taking you shopping. Now come on, let's go," he urged and tugged at her hands with barely restrained impatience.

Anna tried for a good look at his house over her shoulder as he hauled her along. Nice, from what she could see. Neat and clean. Earth tones in the color scheme, that gave it warmth in spite of the amount of white he seemed to like. Although actually the white was sort of nice. Bright. Anna thought it would always look sunny in here, even on the short, dark winter days.

She could see a lot of books and CDs on shelves and wished she could take a closer look. She'd like to know what his tastes ran to. For all she knew, he listened to everything from Mozart to Motorhead. Read legal thrillers. How would she know? She didn't know the first thing about the man who'd just become her lover.

Well, no, she amended silently. That wasn't exactly true. She knew all kinds of things. She knew he was overly fond of the sound of his own voice. Loved to laugh and joke. Was kind to shell-shocked redheads who didn't know how to act after passion burned itself out.

Actually, he'd been more than kind. He'd been gentle, careful with her body and her emotions and concerned about her welfare.

Still, there were many unexplored depths to the man she'd mistaken first for a serious man, then for a shallow buffoon when he opened his mouth and destroyed the dark and dangerous image.

While she mused over the mysteries of the man, he was busy stuffing her into his car. When he climbed behind the wheel, he turned to grin at her like the raving maniac he clearly was.

"If you're good I'll buy you a canoe," he promised, cajoling her.

"What would I do with a canoe?" Anna asked cautiously.

"What would you do with a canoe?" Jay stared at her, then leaned his head out the window and shouted to the sky, "I love this woman!"

He pulled his head back in and took her hand to kiss it.

"What you would do with a canoe, angel, is nothing. Which is why I would buy you one. So I can use it," he explained patiently, as if she should have known that immediately. "But in your case, I think you should keep an open mind about some recreational things," he continued. "You don't know how you'll feel about something until you try it, right? After I've paddled you a few times, you're going to love it." Assurance rang in his voice.

Great. She'd just known spanking was going to come up sooner or later. "I don't think so, Jay."

"You didn't think you wanted to become lovers with me, either, and you're glad you kept an open mind about that, right?"

Well, Anna hated to admit it but he had her there. It was hard, being in the dark about so many things. He had the edge on her. He had all the knowledge and experience. It left her at a distinct disadvantage. Anna silently determined to catch up, pronto, so she could gain some equal footing on these things.

"Right," she agreed cautiously but with a total lack of enthusiasm.

"Trust me." He kissed her hand again and returned it to her lap with a pat.

Trust him. Oh, sure. Right.

"I'll paddle you first. Then I'll show you how to do it and you can paddle me. You look strong enough. It's good exercise and it's fun, I promise," Jay continued with cheerful enthusiasm.

"Great." Her voice said it sounded like anything but.

"Just keep an open mind, okay? Some scientist you are. How do you expect to discover anything with a negative outlook like that?"

Anna sighed inwardly. Well, maybe it was fun. She wouldn't know until she tried, would she? She could try to work up a little enthusiasm. She had wanted to try everything at least once, she reminded herself. The fun things twice. If it wasn't fun, that would be it forever.

"Well, okay. But I think you should be happy I let you tie me up and quit pushing," she informed him grumpily.

Jay stared at her for so long that she started to get nervous about the car staying in the right lane.

"Baby! You mean you want to try it in a canoe? With me?" A broad smile broke over his face. "I knew it. You are one adventurous woman. I knew you were something else. Sure, why not, if that's what you want? Only we'll have to be careful. Lots of the rivers around here are pretty dangerous even for experienced canoeists. We'll pick a safe spot to tie up. Then we'll do anything you want to."

She'd missed something somewhere, Anna realized. She tried to back up cautiously and find out what. "You want to have sex in a canoe?"

He winked joyfully at her. "No, you do. And if you do, I do."

That kind of answer didn't clarify anything.

"You were the one who brought it up," she pointed out, since it was really possible his brain might have gotten shorted out from their highly combustible antics. "You said you wanted to paddle me. You said I'd love it."

Jay eyed her up and down in clear suspicion.

"You don't know anything at all about canoeing, do you? And you're not from around here, are you?"

"No, I don't. And I'm from L.A."

He threw up his hands. "Well, that explains it."

It did? Explained what, exactly? Anna frowned and wondered just how bad her communication skills really were. She'd thought she was improving. "Explains what?"

"Explains your warped ideas about paddling. Honest to God, angel, why would I want to spank you?" Jay demanded in amazement that she could even consider such a thing.

"How should I know? You're the one with all the experience. You're the one who wanted to tie me up," she pointed out indignantly. He was making her sound like some kind of pervert. Just because she didn't have the benefit of his expertise.

"Hey, you loved that, admit it," Jay shot back defensively.

"Yes, I did. You were right. So how do I know a little paddling isn't fun, too?" Anna demanded.

Jay stopped as if to consider that. Finally, he answered her.

"Okay, honey, listen. I'm a fairly broad-minded guy. I'm into variety. I'm willing to experiment. But there are some things…" he trailed off into silence. "All right, if you want me to spank you, I will. But I'd rather teach you to canoe," he finished on a resigned note.

The light dawned slowly but it did eventually dawn.

"You want to teach me to canoe?"

"Yes. It's fun. I think you'd like it, okay?" He gave her a sideways glance. "Look, maybe I'm not like the sophisticated guys you knew in California but obviously I appeal to you more than those alfalfa sprouts ever did because I'm the one you waited for. So I think you could at least give it a try." He paused then added, "If those are the kinds of weirdoes you knew, no wonder you wanted to wait. Sheesh."

Jay reached for her and gave her a one-armed hug. "I can't tell you how glad I am you escaped from that crazy place in one piece," he continued fervently. He shuddered as if considering all the horrors that might have befallen her in the heathen outlands beyond Yankee country. "So I'll buy you a canoe and we'll go paddle together, okay, honey?"

That sounded reasonable. Certainly better than what she'd originally feared he had in mind.

"Okay," Anna agreed meekly.

He smiled warmly at her. "That's my girl." He dropped a quick kiss on her cheek as an added reward.

The car turned down a seemingly endless strip of colonial-style outlet stores. Anna looked in amazement at the decorative wooden signs that named every designer known to man or woman.

Jay saw her reaction and laughed. "Welcome to Freeport, angel."

"This is it?"

"This is it," he agreed. "No neon signs allowed by town ordinance. Neat, huh?"

It was. A shopper's paradise of modern convenience and historic charm in one irresistible package. It was certainly unique and she hadn't had a clue that anything like it existed so close to Portland. No wonder he'd laughed. No wonder he thought she was an idiot for not knowing what he was talking about.

She really didn't get out much.

They parked and Jay pulled her out to walk the last block.

"This is it? L.L. Bean?" Anna asked as they approached the tall white building with green awnings. Outside the world-famous country store, a manmade waterfall cascaded over rocks beside the wide concrete steps.

"This is it," Jay confirmed. He was grinning like a fool at her reaction, black eyes shining with humor and anticipation. He kept her hand in his as he led her up the steps. "Isn't it great?" He beamed at her and Anna thought again that he had a peculiar air of innocent joy. She couldn't help catching his enthusiasm and smiling back.

"Yes, I think it is," she agreed, meaning more than the trip to Freeport. She was beginning to think that maybe, just maybe, he was great.

He had a zest for life that was infectious. He was handsome, fun, gainfully employed and a respectable, tax-paying adult. If he had any major personal flaws like compulsive gambling, drinking or drugs, they were remarkably well-hidden. He was wonderful as a lover, enthusiastic and passionate. He'd made her first experience a good one with his gentle care. And afterwards, he'd been just as considerate and loving with her as he made sure she was unhurt and comfortable.

He'd held her, washed her, brushed her hair and complimented her and then seduced her all over again, making the second time just as good as the first although in a different way. True, he did have a somewhat bizarre sense of humor. But he was also everything she could have asked for and she'd come frighteningly close to discarding him because he happened to claim he was in love with her.

She stopped and said tentatively, "Jay?"

He looked at her expectantly. "What?"

Anna gave him a slow smile and leaned forward to kiss him sweetly and thoroughly. "I think I'm going to like canoes."

Her amethyst eyes glowed with warmth and happiness as they met his ebony depths.

Jay wrapped her in a bear hug and swung her off of her feet. "Glad to hear it, pumpkin."

She frowned. "No pet names referring to my hair. I'll put up with honey, baby, angel and so on but there will be no pumpkin, carrot or flame-top cracks." Firmly, she asserted herself. Even if her feet were dangling off the ground.

His eyes sparkled with wicked glee. "Oh, honey. You know there's one name I have to call you."

She eyed him suspiciously. "What?"

"Jessica Rabbit." He said the name in reverent, worshipful tones that she had to laugh at. And she did bear some resemblance to the voluptuous redhead from *Who Framed Roger Rabbit*.

"You do know who Jessica Rabbit is, don't you, love?" Jay added in an insulting drawl. "You do know what movies are, don't you? Pictures that move and talk?"

She bit his lower lip in mock revenge for that crack. "I do get out sometimes, you know. I don't spend my whole life in my lab. Jane makes me go see movies with her."

"So do Jessica for me," he begged, teasing her.

Anna considered his request. Well, why not? He'd certainly done a lot for her and she hadn't known enough to do the same for him. She had a lot of catching up to do. Meanwhile, if it made him happy, she'd do her best cartoon impersonation.

In a breathy, sexy voice, she indulged him. "I'm not bad. I'm just drawn this way." For good measure, she batted her eyelashes.

His eyes told her that she was bad and just how much he liked her that way.

"I like the way you're drawn," he informed her in heartfelt tones. "You're some piece of, uh, art." The euphemism and his wicked smile told her exactly how he felt about her body.

Anna appreciated the sentiment. Not only was it nice to hear positive things about this new area she was venturing into, she returned the feeling. He was pretty wonderfully bad himself.

"So tell me why this place is always open," she prodded as he pulled her into the store's lobby.

"Because you never know when you might suddenly need to buy a canoe."

Anna had to admit that the store was an experience at any time of the day or night. It wasn't crowded but they weren't the only ones doing some midnight shopping. Roaming through every department with them were shoppers of all ages and from all walks of life. Anna saw everything from tailored suits to well-worn examples of the store's outdoor clothing. The only thing these people might ever have in common was a sudden need to shop for outdoor gear.

Somewhat like herself and Jay, Anna thought soberly. They were about as different as the tweedy matron and the hulking bow hunter ahead of them. What did they really have in common?

They both worked for Frontier. They both sat on the wrong end of Lyle's dreaded lectures. They both lived in Portland. But their areas of interest and expertise couldn't be more vastly different. The same gaping differences extended to their personalities. While she was focused and serious, Jay didn't seem to take anything seriously except birth control. She hid a smile, remembering his uncharacteristic lecture.

Well, maybe that was what she needed in a lover. She was only looking for a playmate, not a partner. She needed to have some fun. She'd been working too hard for too long. Some spontaneous shopping and earthshaking erotic discoveries were exactly what she'd been missing.

And considering how much she was enjoying herself, she was determined not to miss anything else.

"Come on, slowpoke," she urged, tugging playfully at Jay's hand. "I want to look at canoes."

Her new playmate grinned back. "I thought you'd never ask."

Jay wrapped a long arm around her waist and continued, "Since you didn't have flowers, candlelight and violins, the very least I can do for you is buy you the canoe of your dreams. With accessories," he added generously.

"Accessories?" Anna wondered how one accessorized a canoe.

He nodded. "Oh, yes. The right cushions, for example. Comfortable to sit on, but also flotation devices for safety. The right paddles. A wetsuit. All sorts of stuff."

Canoeing was evidently serious business. Anna tried to look suitably impressed.

"Lead me," she invited and leaned into his side.

He was happy to do just that.

Chapter Seven

"Anna. Anna, wake up," a low voice murmured in her ear.

"Not again," she muttered thickly, burying her face deeper into the comfortable warmth that pillowed her head.

A soft laugh answered her protest.

"Come on. You only have to tell me where you live," the voice prodded insistently, and even half-awake she knew it wouldn't let up until she answered.

Anna yawned and complied without fully waking up. She decided she didn't care where she was as long as she could keep sleeping.

Jay looked down at the bright head resting on his shoulder and smiled. She'd fallen asleep on the way back to Portland almost as soon as the car started to move. Lulled by the motion, she'd curled up and snuggled against him like a child. He took it as another positive sign that she'd leaned across the narrow gap between the seats to put her head on his shoulder instead of curling away from him.

He hated to disturb her but he figured she'd want to get ready for work at her own place in the morning, instead of his. So they'd spend what was left of the night there. Tomorrow he'd make sure she had what she needed ahead of time.

It didn't take long to find her townhouse. Since she was beyond waking, Jay fished through her bag until he found her keys. Then he squinted in the light coming from the porch that had been triggered on by the motion of the car as he searched for the one that looked like it fit the front door.

The first try proved his guess correct. Feeling triumphant, Jay left the door open while he returned to the car and gathered one unconscious Amazon up and lifted her clear. She wasn't light but she felt wonderfully good in his arms. In fact, he felt sublimely protective and capable as he carried her inside and kicked the door shut behind them. She could trust him to take care of her. He'd get her safely and comfortably to bed.

In a sudden surge of protective tenderness, he dropped a kiss on her forehead.

She was definitely down for the count. Out cold.

"My princess of passion, I have exhausted you with love," he chortled wickedly.

She didn't even stir.

Since his hostess wasn't about to direct him to her bedroom, Jay followed the traffic pattern and paused to look through doorways as he came to them until he found it.

A little bland. Not what he'd expected of an Amazon's bedroom. Still, considering, he guessed he had proof that she didn't do much in it but sleep.

The thought made his heart swell.

He pulled back the covers, set her carefully down on the bed, then found her alarm clock and set it. While she slept, he undressed her for the second time.

It was more fun when she was an active participant, Jay decided, but this way he could look all he wanted, so there were advantages to both.

She was well worth looking at, too. He couldn't believe a passionate woman so obviously made for love had been untouched.

Blazing red hair made a trail of fire over the pillow and flowed over one breast down to brush at the enticing curve of her hip. Lower, more curls glowed in a fiery covering of feminine heat. A dusky nipple peeked through the whorls of hair that half covered her and he brushed it back to expose both full breasts to his view.

She was a sleeping Venus. As white as marble, but so warm to the touch. As soft as silk under his hands.

No other man had ever seen her like this, he thought as he undressed himself before joining her. It stunned and awed him. He sat on the bed beside her and the mattress dipped, bringing her against his hip.

She sighed softly in her sleep and reached for him.

Jay laid down to gather her in his arms again, marveling at the unexpected gift she'd given him. She shivered and he reluctantly pulled the covers over them both. He consoled himself with the thought that he could touch, even if he couldn't look anymore.

He suited actions to thought and ran his hands over every inch of her curves and valleys. When she responded to his touch even in sleep, he felt deeply gratified. She was like a sleepy cat, arching into his caresses.

Arousal rushed through him. He was abruptly as full of need and as achingly urgent as the first time he'd loved her.

If he wasn't careful, Jay thought his first night with her would also be his last.

She wouldn't be too happy if she woke up raw and aching from his unbridled enthusiasm. Twice in one night was pushing it already. He couldn't take advantage of a defenseless sleeping woman to satisfy his raging adolescent lust.

But he couldn't hold her naked body in his arms and not touch her, either.

"I hope you appreciate this," Jay muttered to her sleeping form as he got up again.

So he couldn't sleep yet. He'd gladly give up a week of sleep for what he'd gained tonight. So he had to wait another day to know the soul-shaking joy of being joined to her fully again. He'd endured more. Been celibate for days. Lots and lots of them. It had been a very long time for him. So he could be deeply thankful his monkish life was over but it wouldn't kill him to do a little more waiting for her sake.

Meanwhile, another unexplored facet of her lay exposed for his discovery — her home.

Jay slid his jeans back on and wandered around. He opened doors and peered into closets. Pulled out drawers and rifled through the contents. Everything was neat and incredibly organized.

"Good," he decided out loud. "You can help me clean my closets out." That way, there'd be room for her stuff.

There was no way they could live in her place. It was too small. Definitely intended for one person. Single occupancy only.

His house, on the other hand, had plenty of room for both of them. Plenty of room for them to grow in, too. He pictured Anna with a dark-haired baby in her arms and smiled. It was just possible that the step toward that future had already been taken tonight.

The future held some changes, that much was certain. He hoped she'd adjust to them fairly easily. One thing he decided had to change right away was her workaholic lifestyle. He'd make sure she came home at night and left work behind on the weekends. She probably just needed a reason. What better reason than himself?

He'd made her scream. He smiled broadly at the memory. Of course she'd want to rush home every night.

He continued through the darkened rooms, turning on lights and poking through the contents each area contained. Her reading material told him a lot. He'd already seen her stack of nonfiction books. The one on being bad he considered a very hopeful sign. Other than that, she had reference books and trade journals. Even, to his amazement, the *Journal of Experimental Mathematics*.

Who in the world would read something like that?

Jay shook his head sadly. Here was a soul crying out for fun.

No personal pictures lay on the tables or hung on the walls. In fact, the walls were heartlessly bare.

A holiday picture of Anna with her assistant was stuck to the refrigerator. Other than that, no Kodak memories anywhere. No old boyfriends, either. Although all things considered, he hadn't really expected any.

The more Jay saw, the more deeply convinced he grew that never, in his entire life, had anyone ever needed him as badly as she did. In fact, in light of the total lack of evidence of the fun and frivolous he found, he didn't think that anyone in the history of humanity had ever been needed as much as he was right then.

It was a good feeling. He didn't think he'd ever been truly needed before.

Jay tiptoed back to bed, his body under control and his curiosity satisfied. He moved carefully to keep from waking her, although that was probably an unnecessary precaution.

His Amazon slept like a log.

He grinned and spooned himself against her sleepy length. She might not love him yet, he reflected, but she needed him. She desired him in a way she'd never desired another man. She wanted him.

For now, it was good enough.

It was a starting point and he'd build from there to teach her lonely heart to love. She deserved to have it all, love and rockets, hearts and flowers, hand-in-hand walks at sunset. Forever.

"Watch out, woman," he told her sleeping form happily. "You've met your match."

The shrilling alarm pierced through the fog of sleep that clouded Anna's mind far too soon. She had just gone to bed, hadn't she? What was wrong with the timer? She groaned in protest and pulled the pillow over her head to block out the sound. She'd been having the most incredible erotic dream and if she could slip back into it she could enjoy the conclusion, something she'd been really close to judging by the pre-orgasmic quivering of her vaginal muscles.

Something was wrong with her pillow, though. It was too narrow. Too hard. And it wasn't cooperating. She opened one eye to find out what the problem was.

The problem, she noticed, was that it wasn't her pillow.

It was an arm.

Not her own arm, either.

While she struggled with that mystery, the arm tightened and hauled her up against a long, solid body. "Mm, good morning, precious," she heard dimly. The shrilling alarm cut off and in the blessed silence, she could hear Jay's heart beating under her cheek. One hand continued the lazy circles around her clitoris that must have inspired the dream. He did have talented hands.

"Did you sleep well? I did." His drowsy voice was lazy with remembered pleasures. Not content to have her against him, he pulled her on top of him and fondled her backside affectionately. His hands cupped her bare cheeks and held her firmly against his morning erection.

Anna immediately lost interest in going back to sleep. The real thing was much more interesting than dreaming about it.

"Anna, Anna. You feel so good." He shifted her slightly, the change in position allowing his penis to slide easily along the vaginal lips that were wet and slick from his arousing caresses.

Well, she thought sleepily. At least he could carry on a conversation for both of them. That was something. She thought he was possibly the perfect lover for a person with poor communication skills.

"I hope you feel as good as I do," Jay continued. Another shift, and his hard tip against her ready opening left her in no doubt about what he meant. He moved his hips to probe gently, seeking entry.

Without thinking, Anna slipped her knees over his thighs and moved against him in response, liking the warm, blunt feel of him.

"Oh, honey." His hands lifted her hips slightly then closed over her buttocks again to haul her downward while he simultaneously pushed up, filling her. She stretched to accommodate him.

"Anna. Oh, Anna. Tell me that doesn't hurt," he pleaded huskily.

"It doesn't," she answered with her eyes still closed and her body still heavy with sleep. He wasn't too big for her at all. He stretched her and filled her and that alone was enough to trigger the pulsing sensation that was starting to feel both familiar and closely associated to Jay.

She was becoming conditioned to him, like Pavlov's dog. Or maybe that should be Pavlov's pussy, in her case. Soon she'd only have to look at his penis and she'd start coming. He wouldn't have to touch her at all. She imagined standing next to him at work, looking at his crotch and trying to stay quiet while orgasm ripped through her and drenched her underwear from the conditioned response to stimulus. The erotic scenario speeded up the pulsing, building toward a peak.

"Good." Relief was evident in his voice.

So was desire.

The single word was her only warning. She found herself abruptly rolled onto her back and then she gained some firsthand experience about "quickies". Hard, fast and furious, he took her from rippling pleasure to violent climax in bare minutes.

He stayed buried in her, pressing deeper inside her and pushing her deeper into the mattress afterwards. She felt taken, claimed, possessed. Her body belonged to his and they both knew it.

"I can't tell you how much I wanted that," he whispered against her hair. "It was all I could do to let you sleep at all last night." The rough ache in his voice would have told her he was sincere, even if the physical evidence of his urgency hadn't.

Anna pondered the implications of that. "You mean you can do this all night?"

Jay smiled warmly at her before he kissed her thoroughly and lazily. Then he answered, "Anytime you feel up to it, baby, I'll be happy to demonstrate."

He braced himself up on one arm to look down at her and brushed her cheek with his fingers. She opened her eyes to meet his.

He looked disgustingly happy. His black eyes sparkled and a shock of hair fell in appealing disarray over his forehead.

"How about tonight?" He made the suggestion hungrily with a wolfish grin.

"Hmm." Anna creased her brow in thought. Was it proper lover's etiquette to spend every night together? She didn't know. Once again, she found herself face-to-face with an abysmal lack of practical knowledge.

"I can't believe you have to think it over. I made you scream," he pointed out smugly.

"You did that just by opening your mouth," Anna grumbled sourly. He was too aggravating to believe.

"In ecstasy, my passion flower," he made the distinction pointedly. "Just the way I'll make you scream and scream again tonight. Forget I even considered leaving a decision of that nature up to you. I've got you in my clutches and you won't escape."

With that, Jay abruptly withdrew from her and stood. For a moment she felt lonely and empty at the sudden loss. Then he reached for her and threw her over his shoulder as if she were a much smaller and lighter woman.

"Come, my beauty," he declared with a piratical laugh. "We need to shower and get dressed. I'll wash your back," he added as incentive when she squirmed and tried to escape his hold.

"Put me down." Anna tried to be firm but it was really very difficult to be assertive while naked and upside down.

"Soon, soon," Jay assured her as he turned on the shower, seemingly in no hurry to relinquish his hold on her.

She delivered a sharp spank to his backside at that and laughed when he roared in surprised outrage at the unexpected assault.

"Oh, you think it's funny, do you?" He set her down and shot her a look filled with dire unspoken threats. "Just wait, precious. Just wait. I'll get you for that."

Anna could imagine how, too. In the most enjoyable way. Maybe, she mused, she should spank him again.

It didn't take long to shower and Jay made good on his promise to wash her back. Funny, she thought. She would have expected the morning after to feel awkward. Especially with a person who was, to all practical intents and purposes, a stranger. Instead, she felt comfortably at ease with him. How could she feel any other way when he was so talkative, so playful and so wonderfully lustful as he let her know in no uncertain way that he was eagerly looking forward to more?

Well, maybe that was normal. How would she know? She was really finding it irritating that he knew what to expect and she didn't. In fact, she'd been offbalance ever since he'd seduced her on his couch before tying her to his bed. She'd expected Jay to be a good lover. She hadn't expected him to be so attentive outside of bed. He'd taken her shopping. He'd obviously carried her inside and put her to bed last night. She couldn't complain about any of it. But what, exactly, had he meant about not leaving decisions up to her?

"Ahem." She made an unsubtle bid for his attention and met his eyes squarely.

"Yes?" Jay turned to look at her with eyes full of admiration. "You want me?" His voice told her that he certainly hoped so, and preferably immediately.

"Turn off your hormones for a minute," Anna instructed, jabbing him in the chest with her index finger. "I want to know what you meant by that remark about 'not leaving decisions of that nature' up to me."

He shot her an incredulous look. "I'm supposed to turn off my hormones when I'm standing in the shower next to a beautiful, naked woman?"

She frowned in warning. "Don't try to change the subject."

"What subject?" All innocence, he shut off the spray, then dug for towels and politely offered her one. He frowned unhappily when she immediately used it to remove his excuse for not paying attention. "Hey, I was enjoying that!" He protested the loss of his view in wounded tones.

Anna ignored his protest. "Come on. I want an answer." She waited expectantly.

Jay hauled her up against himself and took away her towel. "You want an answer? I'll give you an answer." He kissed her deeply and thoroughly and left her speechless. Also breathless. He fondled her various parts for good measure.

"There. Any lightbulbs going on yet, wizard?" He smiled at her, warmth and good humor alive in his eyes.

While she stared blankly at him, he rubbed her dry and turned her toward her closet.

"I hate to say it, sweetheart, but you have to get dressed. We've got work to do today so we can play tonight." He gave her a little push in the right direction.

Anna went, slowly. She noticed that he'd brought a change of clothes for himself. She guessed being lovers involved a certain amount of forethought and planning.

Well, she supposed she'd better get dressed herself. She didn't think she was going to get a better answer out of him now, anyway. For a constant talker, it was irritating that he artfully managed not to say much.

She quickly pulled on underwear and then heard a shocked outcry behind her.

"Haven't you ever heard of Victoria's Secret?"

Hands on her hips, Anna turned to frown at Jay. "These are practical. I'm going to go to work, not out to paint the town red."

He came up, enticingly half-dressed, and tugged at the waistband of her white cotton briefs. "Hm. They do have a certain appeal. I guess you can keep them."

"Thank you, Daddy."

Sarcasm was truly wasted on him, Anna decided. He just winked and blew her a kiss. Why did she bother? She gave up on the impossible man and dressed quickly in jeans and an olive turtleneck. A hasty braid tamed her mane and then a dash of mascara and lipstick finished her routine. She was ready.

She turned to find Jay standing close behind her with a strange expression on his face. "What?" Anna demanded sharply, unnerved by his proximity and intensity.

He reached out to touch her cheek. "Nothing. I just like watching you."

As a matter of fact, he liked everything about her and seeing her in this intimate setting started a funny ache inside. He wanted to know that he would wake up with her every morning. He wanted the right to tease her, laugh with her, love with her. He wanted to hold her and never let her go. He wanted her, all of her, forever.

He didn't think she had any idea how he felt. He'd told her but doubted that it had sunk in. She probably hadn't believed him. She was an objective scientist. Why would she believe in love at first sight?

He loved her with a blinding intensity that had shifted the focus of his entire world from the moment she exploded into view. He wanted to marry her immediately. All he had to do, he mused, was to convince her that it was her idea.

It shouldn't be too hard, he thought. They were so obviously right together. Anna was too smart not to see it, too. And if all else failed he could have Lyle play the shotgun-toting heavy, demanding that she do the right thing.

She was starting to look at him suspiciously, so he quickly distracted her. "Do you have any coffee?"

"No, I don't drink it. Do you want some herbal tea?"

"I want anything you'll give me," Jay informed her. He knew the serious answer would go over her head unnoticed. The woman didn't take him seriously. Maybe he should be reading her books on communication.

"Don't forget your overnight bag," he added as she went to put a mug in the microwave.

"My what?"

He grinned. She was so cute when she was confused. "We're sleeping at my place, so don't forget to bring whatever you'll need."

He could almost see her brain churning before she answered.

"You want me to spend the night at your place?"

"It's the only way to prove that I'm a man of my word," he assured her solemnly, reminding her of his earlier boast.

"Oh."

She gave him a long look before going to pack for the night.

One small step for tonight, one giant step for the future, he decided happily. Before long, her clothes would be hanging in his closets, one item at a time if necessary, and he'd get her moved in without ever having to directly bring it up. The subtle approach.

And he hadn't even begun to use bribery. She wasn't surrounded by a throng of lavish admirers competing with him for her favors but he couldn't count on that happy state continuing. He'd shower her with attention and little presents and she'd be helpless to resist him. She'd be blind to all other men.

It was a very pleasant thought.

Being helpful, he took her bag and carried it to the car when she was ready, tugging her along by the hand.

"I wish you'd stop that," Anna informed him irritably.

"Stop what, sweet?"

"Stop dragging me here, there and everywhere."

He gave her a hurt look. "I'm just making sure you aren't late to work."

"I haven't been late once in three years," she retorted.

"Yeah, I believe that," he mumbled under his breath as he started the car and headed them toward Frontier.

She poked him in the ribs. "What was that?"

He settled that by dragging her close with one arm. "I said, I know how dedicated you are to your work," he answered innocently.

That distracted her. She started mumbling about tests and having something to check today. Jay didn't even try to understand any of it. He just nodded and made agreeable noises whenever it seemed called for.

The only velocity test he was personally interested in involved a certain redhead. She could be as ballistic in his bed as she pleased. Start all the fires she wanted to, as long as she stayed around to put them out. He'd been right. She was one incendiary woman and he was willing to pay any price to keep her.

He'd even go to the lengths of learning to speak whatever foreign language she was rambling on in. Oxidizers, binders, propellant, he had no clue what any of it meant. But it was important to her, so he listened.

All too soon, they arrived. Jay felt like a kid again, wanting to walk her to class so all the other kids would know she was his girl. Well, why not? He twined his fingers through hers and headed toward her lab with her as if it was the most natural thing in the world.

Fortunately, she was lost in some brainy dream world of her own and she probably wouldn't have noticed if he'd ripped her clothes off, let alone walked her to her door.

Jay led her along and continued to throw in the occasional "uh-huh" and "I see" as needed. She was something else. When they reached her lab, he drew her inside, waved to Jane and took Anna's shoulders to get her attention with a gentle shake.

It brought her out of her trance. "What?" she asked, blinking like a sleepwalker.

Instead of an answer, he gave her a good-bye kiss to remember.

"Have a good day, sweetheart. I'll be back to get you for lunch," he informed her.

She still looked confused, so Jay kissed her again lightly and then pushed her toward Jane.

"She's all yours, kid," he called with a friendly wink. "Don't let her set her hair on fire."

He was singing inside all the way to his office, where he found a message from Grant waiting for him. His presence was wanted immediately. Even another royal summons from Lyle couldn't dampen his good mood. Jay strolled to the other man's office full of expansive good feelings.

"Good morning, Lyle," Jay said in a deliberately buoyant voice as he strolled in without knocking.

The fist slamming down on the great desk gave him some idea of what was on Grant's mind.

"Good morning? Good morning? What's good about it, that's what I'd like to know," the man roared in answer.

One meaty paw waved Jay to stand front and center. He complied, hoping Lyle wouldn't get too excited and drop his cigar in the pile of papers that littered the desktop. He didn't see a fire extinguisher anywhere close.

The burly old man looked him up and down with hard eyes. He seemed to know the dramatic effect of a good long pause, too. Jay waited patiently, knowing the answer to that rhetorical question would come sooner or later.

Still, he nearly jumped when Lyle barked out, "So, you kidnapped my head research scientist yesterday afternoon and you decide to bring her back the next morning? Is that what you call burying the hatchet? Is that what you call working with her?"

Ah, he was going to go directly for the throat. Jay played along in the spirit of cooperation.

"No, sir, I—"

"I'd like to know what the hell you do call it!" Lyle's fist made a thunderous, crashing impact with the long-suffering desk again. "I'd like to know what the hell you were thinking!" Crash. "I'd like to know what the hell your intentions are toward my Anna, you damned two-bit Romeo!" Crash. Pause. Puff.

Enough cigar smoke billowed around his grizzled head to make him look like the admissions clerk for hell.

"Yes, sir, I—"

"Don't think you can play around with her like some damned kind of toy! She's not some plaything to amuse yourself with and discard, you damned skirt-chasing reprobate!" Crash.

Jay began to wonder if the bumps and dents in the desk's battered surface where all the result of Lyle's ham-handed fist-banging lectures.

Impressive, if true.

"No, sir, she—"

Lyle wasn't ready to let him answer for himself yet, Jay noticed as he was interrupted once again.

"Don't you talk to me about any damned, so-called modern liberated uncommitted long-winded disguise for not growing up and facing up to a man's responsibilities!" Crash, the fist slammed down again.

The old man was truly in rare form today, Jay noticed admiringly. He put energy, enthusiasm and heart into a lecture. That kind of enthusiastic performance demanded an appreciative audience. He made an effort to stand in what he hoped was a suitably chastened position and even made a good try at hanging his head.

That seemed to fire Lyle up even more.

"And don't you humor me, you half-grown untrained puppy!" The lit cigar threatened a lampshade, the "out" tray and a bookshelf in one sweeping motion. "You pay attention, you hear me, boy?"

"Yes, sir, I—"

"Damned right!" Crash. Glare. Puff. "Now I want you to start talking and I want you to make it good, because you owe me one hellacious explanation!" he roared on.

If only Grant would expend his energy on the right person, Jay thought wistfully. He'd like to see Anna stand up under this raging, fist-banging, smoke-blowing tirade and explain why she didn't want to do the right thing by him.

Although to be fair, he hadn't proposed. The discouraging response to his declaration of love had convinced him to wait. Finding out he was serious had changed her mind about the wisdom of becoming lovers and only his quick action and practiced skill had saved him.

He'd seduced her, gotten her limp and mindless with pleasure and proceeded to get her out of her clothes and into bed before she had time to reconsider. It had worked but it had been close. Far too close for comfort. And judging by the fact that she'd had to think about whether or not to spend the night with him tonight, he could see that he had a long campaign ahead.

Still, Jay thought he did have some advantages. He knew what women liked, from long experience as a skirt-chasing reprobate before his reformation. And he was her first lover. No matter how she rationalized that one, it had to mean something. He intended to see to it that she never wanted to go looking for a replacement, either.

Yes, he reflected, he'd keep her so satisfied she'd be too exhausted to wander. And once the three months of automatic birth control were up, they could talk about babies.

The thought of creating a life with her made his heart soar. He was a greedy man. He wanted it all. Love. A family. Commitment. Happily ever after. A few little minor obstacles like Anna's total lack of interest in those things didn't discourage him. From the lack of family pictures and cards around, he didn't think she knew what she was missing, so how could she know if she wanted it?

"Sir," he began, seeing that Lyle really was finally going to let him say something, "I didn't kidnap her. I took her to lunch, since you did suggest that we come to an understanding."

That seemed to fire the other man up again.

"I'd like to know what the hell kind of understanding it took all afternoon and night to come to!" Grant roared, banging on the desk some more in a timpani burst.

"Sir, I—"

"Do you take me for an idiot? Do you think I'll believe nothing happened?" An accusing stab of the cigar threatened Jay's favorite power tie.

"Of course not," he answered readily. That admission, however, added fuel to the fires of indignation that were burning high enough as it was, instead of serving to damp them down.

"So you admit it, you damned satyr! I'd like to know what the hell you're going to do with—"

"Grant!"

The volume got through where reason and politeness failed, Jay observed with satisfaction as he successfully cut the other man off. No wonder Anna had finally stooped to throttling the man with his own tie. Her actions that night were making more sense all the time.

He waited until he had his full attention. Then he went on, "I intend to marry her, to answer your question. Obviously, she'll continue her work. I doubt that anything could drag her away from it." That was an understatement. As it was, Jay had visions of a working honeymoon. Why not, as long as he got the bride. "We did come to an understanding of sorts but there are one or two small details to reconcile before the happy occasion."

Grant glared at him in suspicion and blew more smoke his way. "What details?"

"Well, she isn't overly thrilled with the idea. In fact, I think it's safe to say that marriage is the last thing on her mind right now. I left her raving about some Freedom Finale she's messing around with."

That distracted Lyle for a moment. "She's got something?"

"I think so, yes. At least, something to test. I didn't understand much of what she said, to be honest."

Grant snorted. "Who could? Doesn't matter. She'll do it, all right. Now what's this about you two?" He made another stabbing gesture with the cigar, perhaps to indicate that if Jay didn't continue his explanation promptly, he'd light another one.

Perish the thought.

Jay shuddered internally and continued rapidly, "I have a plan. Before she knows what hit her, she'll suddenly decide marriage was her idea and she'll be out to haul me down the aisle."

Lyle Grant gave another snort, this one clearly indicating sheer disbelief.

"Leave it to me," Jay assured him. "She's no match for my sneaky, conniving ways. She's far too honest to ever suspect how low another person could go to get what they want."

A slow, unwilling smile creased Grant's face.

It looked like it hurt.

"That's my boy," he rumbled, looking like a smiling warthog. "You see to it that she does change her mind or I'll have to give her a good talking-to. What the hell kind of life it is to do nothing but work, work, work, I don't know. You see that she takes more time off, you hear me?"

Jay heard. As much as it would do his heart good to be a witness to his Amazon getting the lecture of her life on the subject of her duty to do right by him and save him from a life of sin, he wasn't too sure it wouldn't backfire.

No, he thought, she was too ready to fight to simply fall in line if he told her they were getting married. He thought the key to her heart was a soft sell. A less-than-subtle demonstration of all the joys awaiting her as his cherished life-long companion. He thought he just might get somewhere planting the suggestion and letting the idea grow until she accepted it as her own.

Cockily, he assured Lyle through the haze of smoke, "Leave her to me, sir. I'll make an honest woman of her and make sure she learns how to have fun, too."

Chapter Eight

If Anna had hoped to dive into work and ward off Jane's interrogation, it was a very short-lived hope.

One look at the snapping blue eyes and tapping foot told her she'd have to wait to try her idea for the Freedom Finale's blue shower.

Jane was going to drag it all out of her sooner or later. She might as well make it sooner and get it over with. Still, Anna made herself some tea to postpone the inevitable at least slightly.

How did lovers handle public curiosity? Make an announcement? Be seen together and let people draw their own conclusions? Considering that they'd been seen leaving the building together for lunch the day before and her car had remained overnight, coupled with the fact that they hadn't returned until the following morning, she thought it had to pretty much amount to a very public announcement.

She hated to admit it but the mouthy man was right, after all. They couldn't keep their relationship a secret and it was probably already making headlines, at least on office e-mail.

So much for her chance to explore, experiment and play the field. She'd gone and gotten herself trapped from square one. She supposed there were worse fates, though. At least she'd trapped herself with an interesting, attractive, attentive and virile lover.

Anna heard Jane clear her throat expectantly in a ploy for attention. She gave up diligently stirring her lemon and rosehip tea. She'd postponed as much as could be hoped for already. At least, she thought, the vitamin C would help buffer her. It promised to be a somewhat stressful day.

"Okay, ask," Anna said before she turned around to face the music.

"Ask?" Jane batted innocent lashes. "What would I want to ask you about? Gosh."

"Sarcasm doesn't suit you."

Jane grinned unrepentantly and waved for her to sit down. "Tell me everything. Did you remember to take notes? He must have passed some test at lunch, considering you never came back. I already know you're seeing him again, because he said he was taking you to lunch today. Another long one?"

Her assistant was bubbling over with as much excitement as a child on Christmas morning.

"I've decided I sort of like him a little," Anna said nonchalantly as she sipped her tea.

"Sort of? A little? Whoa, I'd say that's the understatement of the century," Jane crowed. She bounced over and perched on Anna's desk. "So? Talk."

Anna talked.

"Well, we had lunch and I asked him if he'd had a blood test."

Blue eyes widened to the size of saucers. Anna had heard the expression before but had never seen an example close up in real life. It was gratifying. Also a little alarming. Maybe that hadn't been the right thing to do.

"Was that wrong?" Anna asked a little hesitantly. "I thought you were supposed to ask."

Jane gave her a thoughtful look. "Wrong? No, but most people wouldn't have. Considering you'd just met him, though, it was reasonable to want to know."

That was a relief. "Good," she said with feeling. "I was starting to wonder. He choked and coughed a lot."

Something suspiciously like laughter burst out of her assistant. "Oh, dear." Her eyes glistened with mirth.

It was funny, Anna realized. She decided to skip the details of what happened after that and sum it up. "So, well, that's all. I think. And he made me go to L.L. Bean in the middle of the night to buy a canoe. Is that normal?"

"A canoe?" Jane shot her a look of sheer amazement. Just when Anna had thought she'd surprised her beyond further surprises already. "Let me get this straight. Did he buy you a canoe?"

"Yes. At first I thought he meant something else when he started talking about paddling but when I realized he just wanted to give me canoe lessons, I was so relieved that I agreed," Anna answered. "Why?"

Jane looked at her for a long minute. "Anna, he's an avid canoeist."

"How do you know that?" Anna asked, although she couldn't see what it had to do with anything if he was.

"I have my sources. When you nearly did him on your desk, I made it my business to find out everything about him. Listen, when a man buys you jewelry, it can be pretty vague. It could mean, I'm sorry. Or it could mean thanks and let's do it again. Or even thanks, and good-bye. But when a man who loves to canoe buys you one, it only means one thing." Sober knowledge wiped the smile from the face that only moments ago had been laughing.

It made Anna distinctly nervous.

"What?" she demanded with worried sharpness.

"It means that I should go buy a dress that will make me look fat and that I'll never wear again," Jane replied.

"Huh?" That made no sense at all, Anna thought.

"You know, it's an old tradition that bridesmaid dresses are unattractive. Anna, the man bought you a canoe. He plans to make you a convert to all his favorite activities. He doesn't just want to sleep with you. He wants to keep you. This is beyond serious. You might as well start shopping for your trousseau."

Serious? That serious? Anna stared back at Jane in mixed surprise and dismay. Maybe she'd heard wrong. "Serious?"

Jane nodded soberly.

Well. She now knew where she could always shop anytime she needed to, she reflected in an attempt to find a bright side. And it was just the kind of place to find almost anything she might need to survive Jay being serious. They specialized in survival gear.

Anna raised stricken violet eyes to Jane's. "I just wanted to have fun. Try new things. It was just canoeing." She sounded as woebegone as a child who'd accidentally broken something she'd only meant to look at. "I didn't know. Now what do I do? Should I give his canoe back?"

Jane patted her hand. "Don't worry about it, boss. Let's go blow something up instead. It'll make you feel better."

"But—"

"It'll be all right," Jane assured her soothingly. "He seems very nice and very fond of you. I'm sure the two of you will be very happy together."

Anna let out a faint whimper.

Happy. Together. With an egomaniac, a compulsive talker, a disturbed midnight shopper who'd never let her sleep through the night again. He couldn't even bring himself to call her by her real name. She'd be answering to a whole string of his stupid little endearments for the rest of her days. Their children would grow up thinking her real name was sweetie-pie or some godawful thing.

She slumped over her desk and decided something like this was too much to doctor with a little vitamin C.

She'd outdone herself this time. What exactly had she been thinking? That she could just learn the rules of social behavior and how to deal with the opposite sex in two days? Well, she hadn't. Instead, she'd gotten herself involved with a man and his canoe and she still didn't even understand what the canoe had to do with anything.

Maine was certainly different.

Well, Anna decided firmly, she couldn't do anything about him or his canoe now. So she might as well get busy with the kind of chemistry she could control. Today, she would make the prototype Freedom Finale. Or, at least, stay sufficiently occupied in a sufficiently demanding task to be able to avoid thinking.

Jay was at least right about that much. Thinking had gotten her into trouble.

It was easier than she expected to throw herself into it and lose herself in the task. The morning flew by. In no time at all, her annoying, aggravating, sticking-his-canoe-in-where-it-damn-well-didn't-belong nemesis was back, looking oh-so-innocent. As if he hadn't just turned her entire orderly existence upside down as carelessly as he'd thrown her over his shoulder that morning.

Jay draped himself over her workbench and eyed her in a way that told her he was mentally undressing her and proceeding to do a whole lot more.

She glowered at him.

He smiled cheerily at her.

"Hey, luscious, come here and kiss me," he invited, wiggling his brows in a way that she guessed was supposed to either make her laugh or sizzle with desire, she wasn't sure which.

"I don't feel like it," she muttered sulkily.

"Okay. I'll come and kiss you." Undeterred, the thick-skinned man suited actions to words and swept her up into a dramatic dip to give her a cinema-style kiss.

At least, Anna thought, there were some consolations to the affair. She drank in the heady pleasure kissing him provided. His lips were warm and sweet on hers and the scrape of his jaw excitingly hard and rough against her smooth skin.

The kiss ended and Jay restored her to an upright position. He frowned at her less-than-deliriously-happy expression. "Baby, that is not the face of a happy woman. What's the matter, didn't your binder or whatever work?"

Anna leaned into him and sniffed. "I don't have a problem with chemistry in the lab."

"You don't have a problem with chemistry outside the lab, either, believe me," he declared in earnest.

"That's not funny."

He patted her back and hugged her comfortingly. "Now I know something went wrong or you'd be laughing gaily at my stunning wit. Maybe you're just hungry. Let's get some lunch, you'll feel better."

Maybe he was right. Maybe, she thought, brightening a little, he'd play footsies with her under the table. Certainly he'd kiss her some more.

"Okay." She leaned against his side and he wrapped an arm around her waist as they walked. "Or maybe we could go to a little hotel you know."

She was now officially really, really bad, she thought in satisfaction. She'd suggested it. And she hoped he'd agree.

It took Jay by surprise, evidently. He nearly stumbled and then gave her a questioning look. "Is my amazing Amazon propositioning me? I might have to accept. It wouldn't be polite to turn a lady down."

"Yes, I'm definitely propositioning you," Anna announced. If he could do it, she could, she defended internally. Besides, it was sounding better all the time. She had an awful lot of time to make up for, after all. Who knew? She certainly hadn't. If she'd known what she was missing, she would have offered to buy him first.

"I am hungry, though," she added as they walked. "Maybe we could do both. Aren't there things we haven't tried with food?"

Jay gave her a long, lust-filled look. "Oh, honey. There are all kinds of things we haven't tried. But I think I'd better stick to feeding you for now."

"Oh?" She felt disappointed. She'd heard about lunch hour rendezvous and she wanted to have one.

"Yes. You'll need your strength tonight." His black eyes promised unspeakable delights that would go on as long as she could stand. Then sit. Then lie.

She shivered in delightful anticipation. Well, he did have a point there. She brightened slightly, thinking about the coming evening. If they ate now, they could skip dinner and just get right to it.

Then she realized what she was thinking and turned worried amethyst eyes to his. "Jay, do you think I'm abnormal?"

He eyed her cautiously. "In what way, precious?"

"Stop with all the names. I mean, is it abnormal to want to have sex with you all the time?"

"No," he assured her firmly. "It's very normal. Really. Absolutely. Couldn't be better." He paused then added, "But I wish you'd stop saying that. It isn't sex."

She looked back at him questioningly.

The heck with it, he decided. The sooner she faced up to it, the better. She had to get over her phobia about the "L" word. "It's called making love, sweetheart. It's not just an exercise. It's what two people who want to be close to each other and share their innermost selves do. Sex is what strangers do in hotel rooms. Okay?"

She didn't look like she'd gotten the point, he decided. She looked confused. In a way, he was glad. If he had his way, she'd never know anything but making love and she could call it anything she wanted to. She could call it Doing It, the horizontal mambo, mattress dancing or flat-out animalistic fucking. As long as she continued to enjoy it with him and nobody else.

"Never mind, honey." Jay hugged her again as they reached his car. "Call it anything you want to. But it's special," he told her seriously as he smoothed back her hair. One fiery tendril had escaped the confines of her braid and it wound around his finger as if even her hair wanted to be closer to him. He liked that idea. He felt that way himself.

Special? Anna pondered that. She supposed he was right. Even she knew he'd been unusually sensitive and caring. She'd heard enough to know that as great as it had been with Jay, sex wasn't always great. It could even be awful, although it was impossible to imagine feeling awful with Jay touching her. It was impossible to imagine feeling anything but good, better and ecstatic. That was certainly special.

"Stop," Jay teased her, "I can see your brain spinning from here. We're just two lovers going to have lunch. Quit thinking about it and get in so we can go do it."

"Just lunch, right? No canoes involved anywhere?" Anna asked with a look of dark suspicion.

He wasn't even going to ask, Jay decided. California must be one weird place.

"No canoes," he promised. "Come on, love. Kiss me again and smile."

She did.

Then she raced him, hopping in and slamming the door as they simultaneously leaped into their seats.

"I won," she informed him, sure she'd made it a split second ahead.

He gave her a look of mocking wisdom. "It's not whether you win or lose."

"No?"

"No." Jay shook his head to emphasize his point and leaned closer to brush kisses on her face. "It's how you play." His lips teased the corner of her mouth and his tongue flicked sweetly over hers. Then he drew away before she could fully kiss him back.

"Oh." Anna pretended to think that over seriously. Then she gave him a hard, deep, longing kiss to prove her dedication to play. One of the things she loved about being his lover was the total freedom to take the lead, or follow his, as she chose. She didn't know which was more fun—being the aggressor and tying him in knots of desire or being happily tied up herself.

It was all fun and she was going to take his advice and enjoy it. Anna trailed off the kiss and ended by blowing in his ear for the memories it would invoke.

He smiled at her. "I think you're learning."

"I think you're right," she agreed.

"But you forgot to tell me what you wanted," he sighed in disappointment.

"You mean…" Anna leaned over his side, traced the outline of his earlobe with her tongue and murmured throatily, "What I want for lunch?"

Jay laughed. "Precious, you're really learning. You made a joke."

She curled against him with her head on his shoulder during the short ride, enjoying just being close to him for some inexplicable reason.

He fed her his french fries in between French kisses over their table and played footsies with her under it. He teased her and just generally made her feel good. Anna was thoroughly cheered up by the time he talked her into sharing a brownie sundae with him.

They took turns taking bites and feeding each other, sharing the same spoon, which Jay solemnly claimed made it taste better.

Anna paid him back by nodding and launching into a long and technical sounding explanation for the physics of flavor and how emotions color perception just to be contrary.

She verbally unmanned him and left him dazed. He didn't know how to take her.

Ha. What was she worried about? She could handle him, canoe or no canoe. She just needed to spend more time thinking positively. Saying affirmations. All the recent changes were a strain on her newfound confidence, that was all, Anna decided firmly.

She silently recited a list of her positive credits to herself as she fed him the last bite of brownie in a sudden fit of generosity. That he'd managed to lighten her mood had nothing to do with it, she told herself.

It was simply selfishness. She wanted him in his best form for his coming demonstration of endurance. She wanted him doing his worst in his wickedest way for as long as possible. She smiled happily, just imagining the sensual marathon. No matter who collapsed first, she felt serenely confident that they'd both thoroughly enjoy themselves.

She was looking forward to it. And he wouldn't be taking off in the middle of the night tonight, she decided. She'd wear him out and leave him too drained and exhausted to even think about canoes or whatever came next.

Jay returned her to her lab and opened the door with a bow, sweeping his arm to indicate her way. With a sexy wink, he murmured, "My fireball of passion, my flame of desire, I'll see you at five."

Anna frowned at the distinctly redhead references. "Go away," she growled.

He gave her a pitying glance and shook his head sorrowfully. "Anna, Anna," he sighed. "What will it take for you to admit you want me to stay?"

With that parting shot, he was gone.

But only in person.

He'd left something behind. The most outrageous, enormous bouquet of flowers she'd ever seen. In fact, it looked like an arrangement for somebody's funeral. Hers, she couldn't help thinking.

She looked questioningly at Jane.

"They came right after you left for lunch," Jane answered with a distinct smirk. "It looks like your man wants to say it with flowers."

Great. What was he saying? Nothing in her communication research mentioned interpreting flowers. Body language, tone of voice, yes. Flowers, no.

Maybe he was threatening to bury her in flower petals.

Then it occurred to Anna that Jane was still there. "You haven't been here this whole time, have you?" she asked in sudden concern.

She hoped she hadn't taught her bad habits to Jane. If she had, she'd just have to reform her. There would be no more workaholics in her lab. New policy.

Jane answered that with a very wide grin. The Cheshire type. "Nooo," she drawled wickedly. "I had lunch with Eldon."

"Eldon?" Anna gave her an inquiring look.

"Eldon," Jane confirmed. "Hey, I think he's kind of cute. Those wire-rimmed glasses, the pocket protector…" Jane let her voice trail off suggestively.

Anna was amazed. Jane and Eldon? "You think an accountant is sexy?"

"I think he's sweet. Kind of shy. Very intelligent."

Hmm. Maybe Jane needed a new mother hen project now that Anna was flying the coop. Who would have guessed she'd pick Eldon? The more Anna thought about it, though, the more she thought the two just might be a good match after all. Jane would keep conversation going, keep things lively and get Eldon into the swing of things. And Eldon would settle Jane down. She thought her assistant just might be in for a surprise or two, there. Eldon might be shy but he was anything but a pushover.

Shaking her head in wonder at the newest development, Anna stepped around the ominous, looming floral arrangement from a decorator's nightmare and poked through the abundant foliage for a card.

She found it.

"Passion flower: tulips are red, irises are blue, you're going to scream before I'm through."

A little heart accompanied the verse. He was one bad poet. The rhyme matched the flowers for taste.

Then Anna took a closer look at the loud bouquet and realized that it included the tulips and irises mentioned in the poem, as well as daisies. Red, white and blue. Understanding dawned. He'd actually been listening that morning. He was wishing her good luck on her test. Amazing.

In his oh-so-unsubtle way he was trying to encourage her efforts.

She also thought he was trying to bring his playful attitude into her work. She shook her head faintly, a rueful smile curving her mouth.

Just when she thought he was truly too aggravating to believe, he turned around and proved himself genuinely endearing.

Jay bounded into his office full of expansive good feelings for life and all his fellow creatures. Anna had kissed him. Anna had laughed and teased and blown in his ear again. He thought he was making progress.

He did a little soft-shoe step as he rounded the desk and made a sweeping bow to a startled Eldon, who'd evidently been waiting for him.

"Eldon, my good man! What can I do for you?"

The mild accountant eyed him seriously. "Jane said you and Anna are seeing each other. She said it's serious."

Jane had said that? How gratifying. Jay smiled. He'd thought she was on his side but he hadn't been absolutely sure. Another unexpected bonus in his favor. With Jane reminding his reluctant love of his good points, she'd be harassed continually.

Wonderful.

"I told you she likes me," Jay informed the doubter smugly. "Miss Firecracker is lighting up my nights and coloring my world. I knew she was meant to be Ginger to my Fred." He danced over to his chair and sat, feet propped on his desk, hands steepled together below a satisfied smile.

Eldon still looked doubtful, Jay noticed. Some people took more convincing than others. Which reminded him.

He dug through his desk then jumped up again to rummage in a file cabinet.

"What are you looking for?"

"My favorite redhead's records," Jay answered smoothly. "I have all the personnel files here somewhere. I pulled them while I was putting together Frontier's big picture for the new marketing plan. Obviously I didn't look closely enough at hers. I think I should take a closer look now. There's bound to be all sorts of useful information in there."

"I don't think you're supposed to do that," the other man replied cautiously.

Jay wasn't listening. He pulled the desired folder free with a triumphant shout and started to leaf through it.

"Here! This is exactly what I was talking about," Jay announced, waving a sheet of paper in Eldon's general direction. "It's as bad as I thought. Worse."

"What is?"

"Her IQ. Look at this. No wonder she doesn't have fun. No wonder she takes things too seriously. No wonder she's confused about what she wants. She's not just a genius, she's about twenty points above that." Jay frowned in disgust at the information.

"I don't think you're supposed to look at that." Eldon sounded slightly alarmed.

Jay shot him an impatient look. "What am I going to do? Alert Mensa? They probably already know about her. Relax."

Eldon straightened his glasses on his nose. "How can you say she doesn't know what she wants? She's brilliant."

Jay shook his head sadly. "Eldon, Eldon. Pay attention. She's not just brilliant, she's a certified mega-genius. That's exactly the problem. She thinks too much."

Eldon looked increasingly befuddled.

"Consider Einstein," Jay suggested. "Brilliant when it came to things like the theory of relativity, right? But the man got lost going from his lab to his house. Just like you-know-who. She should stick to what she's good at and leave managing the relationship to me."

Eldon looked thoughtful in a confused sort of way.

Jay patted his shoulder soothingly. "It's like this," he explained. "Love is very simple. You meet, you fall in love, you stay together forever in disgusting bliss. Simple, right? But she doesn't think that way. Her mind is very complex, so she tries to make a simple thing complicated and it isn't."

"It isn't?" echoed the other man.

"No. It isn't. But fortunately, she's distracted with her little toys right now and if I can keep it that way, she'll be living in disgusting bliss before she stops to realize what happened." Jay rubbed his hands together in delight at the thought and barely refrained for chortling evilly at the thought of trapping her in his loving snare.

His plan was a simple one. Keep her busy. Keep her working during the day and delightfully worn out during the night. Keep her hopping off balance. She wouldn't have time to analyze anything to death. And when she did stop to think, hopefully he'd have a chance to see that what she thought about was heavily influenced and artfully suggested by himself.

Yes, everything was going to work out perfectly. It couldn't be going better. She'd even admitted that she wanted him all the time. He wanted to jump for joy and could barely contain his euphoria.

She was falling for him. He was sure of it.

With an effort, Jay dragged his attention back to the present. "Was there something you wanted to see me about?" he asked Eldon curiously.

To his surprise, the man actually, definitely blushed. He sat up taller, straightened his tie and readjusted his wire-rimmed glasses.

"Uh, I wanted to ask your advice about dating," he said shyly.

"Hello, my proud beauty," drawled the black-haired and no doubt black-hearted man who stood posing in her doorway. His business suit didn't keep him from looking or sounding like a villain bent on ravishment.

Anna looked him over and wondered where he'd gotten his penchant for dramatics.

She half-expected him to wave a property deed in front of her nose and threaten to tie her to the railroad tracks in front of an oncoming train if she wouldn't submit to his wicked advances.

Still, she didn't want to be rescued from him. His wicked advances were far too enjoyable. Earth-shattering. Soul-shaking. Mind-expanding beyond anything. Exciting.

Who would settle for a hero when she could have the wicked black-hearted villain? She didn't think traditional heroes knew about things that could be done with whipped cream. She was certain Jay did. In fact, having been tied down by him once, she was considering refusing to submit for the fun of repeating the experience.

The fun things, after all, she did want to do twice. And it had been fun.

Her villainous lover was looking distinctly disappointed. "What? No reply?"

Anna decided it was time she asserted herself and took the lead with him again.

She held his eyes as she began to slowly, seductively, unbutton her lab coat. For a beginner, she thought she did fairly well. She shrugged out of the concealing garment, one shoulder at a time then let it slide down and fall to the floor. Then she stretched in a lithe, sinuous movement that had her full breasts straining against the confines of her form-fitting knit top.

His eyes were bulging, she noted in satisfaction.

She let her arms drop to her sides and moved toward him with a distinct sway to her hips. She kept coming until she was right up against him, wound his tie around one hand and yanked his head toward hers for a searing kiss. The grip held him still as she teased him. She ran her tongue over the outline of his mouth, nipped and bit at his lips and then finally captured him in a deep, wet kiss to send his heart into overdrive.

When she released his mouth, she said in a velvety soft, dangerous voice, "You're late."

He looked dazed.

"You said five," she continued. "It's two minutes after." Still holding him by his tie, she used it like a leash and led him through the door and started down the hall. "I am very disappointed. Is this how you keep your word?"

She teased him by brushing the soft curve of her breast against him while they walked. Then she delivered her next challenge. "I hope you do better with your other promise." Dark threat colored her honeyed voice. "Don't disappoint me again."

Her sensual teasing left him in no doubt about her meaning. She was ready to play with a vengeance.

Anna realized she might have overdone the teasing when he grabbed her by the waist, threw her over his shoulder and ran to the parking lot.

He set her down and leaned full-length against her as he pushed her against the car door and trapped her with his body, letting her feel intimately his reaction to her words. He was magnificently engorged. Anna wanted to touch that erection, toy with his...cock. She wondered if she had the nerve to say the word *cock* out loud and if Jay would like it. He made her feel a mind-bending combination of tender emotion and raunchiness.

"I won't disappoint you, love," Jay promised. He ran his hands up under her shirt and inside her bra. He boldly caressed her breasts and teased her hard nipples, pinching them lightly between his fingers. His knee nudged her legs apart and rode up to press into her crotch. Anna instantly wanted to spread her legs wide for him and invite him to slide his hand inside her pants and make her come right then and there. "I'll love you until you can't walk," he vowed. "Then I'll love you till you can't stand. I'll make you scream and beg for mercy." Heat glittered in his ebony eyes.

So this was what it felt like to make out in a parking lot. Anna was in heaven. The urgency was thrilling and so was the knowledge that they could be caught by someone else coming along. She loved the sensations he created reaching under her clothes. It was somehow more exciting than when she was naked. It felt distinctly clandestine and forbidden and it turned her on to an unbelievable degree.

Villains were wonderful.

Jay cupped her breasts and squeezed gently. Then one hand moved down between her thighs to boldly cup her mons and Anna leaned back against the car to stay standing. Any minute now he was going to unzip her jeans and rub his thumb over her aching clit, penetrate her with his fingers and she was going to come right there, right in front of anybody who might walk by. Anybody could watch her spread her legs and moan while she got banged in public because she was not about to tell Jay to stop.

Besides, the parking lot was practically empty and the angle of Jay's body shielded her from view. They were probably the only ones still there, he really could just do it, do her…

"Get in the car, precious," he ordered in a soft voice. She shivered in delight. He was as close to the brink as she was.

He made the drive to his house in record time, in spite of the impediment of driving with her hands under his suit and her tongue in his ear. He parked, hauled her out of the car and ran with her to the door. While he fumbled with the lock and key, Anna took advantage of his preoccupation to unbutton his shirt all the way, pull it open and lick his flat male nipples.

She was feeling villainous herself.

Jay finally managed to get the door open and dragged her inside and down to the floor. She landed on top and continued to unbutton, unfasten and tear at his clothes. In the spirit of fair play, he helped with hers. He got her shirt up and tore her bra free to bare her curves to his hungry lips and hands.

Jay's mouth on her sent a jolt of electric shock through her and Anna cried out softly, arching her back to thrust her chest up to him to offer herself more fully.

She dimly heard his low, triumphant laugh as he pushed her down and hauled her shirt over her head. She reached for him blindly, wanting it all and wanting it now, but he evaded her.

"Jay," she groaned in an agony of need, "I want you. Now. Right now, Jay." There was no teasing in her words this time, only raw urgency.

Then he was there, over her and her clothes were gone.

"I'm here, baby," he whispered. He kicked free of his pants and closed his hands over her aching breasts.

She was lost in a world of burning, aching, empty need and only he could fill it. She arched against his weight, seeking his full possession. Her legs curled around his and she moved until she found his hardness. "Now," she sobbed, as his hot tip pressed lightly between her legs. "Now, Jay, please, please," she begged. She was beyond caring about anything but the emptiness inside her that cried out for him to fill her.

He held back and she strained against him wildly, succeeding in gaining a little of him as the tip probed her ready opening but it wasn't enough. Not nearly enough. He refused to give her more and she sobbed in frustration. "Jay!"

He hesitated a moment. Then a shudder went through his frame and he plunged into her deeply.

She screamed.

"Like that?" His hoarse whisper against her ear added to the shivers of sensation running through her. He pinned her flat so she couldn't move against him or shift to take him more deeply.

"Please. Please." She trembled beneath him. "Oh, Jay, please." Her need was a torment that threatened to break her into a thousand aching pieces.

"Everything," he promised, lifting her to cup and hold her bottom to bury himself further. She gasped at the feel of him pressing deeply and clenched her legs around his hips to try to hold him. "I'll give you all of it, everything you want," he added in a low, rough voice.

She closed her eyes and strained in his grasp but he held her still and wouldn't let her move and refused to move himself.

Anna waited, knowing she was too lost to fight him, helpless with need. She shook with the force of it. And suddenly she understood what he was doing. He was dominating her sexually, demanding her surrender. He wasn't going to let her find satisfaction until she gave it. Anna made the decision without thinking, relaxing into him, no longer struggling to take control of the situation or retain any control over herself.

Then and only then he relented and gave her what she needed, filling the emptiness and pouring himself into her in a wild, violent frenzy. Each plunging stroke brought a cry from her until she was sobbing and screaming in mingled ecstasy and continued need. He purposely drew it out, holding back and making it build until she thought she'd die if she didn't find release.

Then it came and he rode with her through the storm.

Spent, he carefully rolled to his back and brought her on top of him, staying deeply inside her. Her tears ran down his chest and she continued to shake from the force of emotion and the violence of her climax.

Finally, she lifted her head and raised wounded eyes to his. "You made me beg," she accused, hurt. "You made me need you and you made me beg." Her real complaint, unvoiced, was understood perfectly by both of them. He'd pushed past an inner barrier. She'd not only let him, she'd taken it down and thrown it aside and there was no going back from that. No retreat to safety.

"Yes," he agreed. He pulled her down and kissed her softly. He tasted the salt of her tears and licked the trail in an animal caress.

Jay stood with her and carried her to the bed, then laid her down and pushed himself into the cradle of her hips. He was already full and heavy with need again and he pressed against her softness in a sensual prelude.

"Why?" Why hadn't it been enough for him to have her as his lover, why had he demanded everything she was with nothing held back so she could never be without him and be whole again?

"Shh, love."

He slowly entered her again and Anna closed her eyes to feel the incredible sweetness his deepest touch gave her. Tears still ran down to wet her hair and he brushed them away.

"Shh, baby. Don't cry." His tender whisper against her cheek was a soothing caress.

"It's not fair, Jay," she protested in a raw voice.

"Shh. Quiet, love."

Slow, soothing hands explored and pleasured every inch of her in a gentle taking and Anna quieted as he soothed shattered nerves and brought her down from the overstimulated state that had made pleasure almost pain.

"That's it," he encouraged when she responded fully to him, curling into him and moving with him. "That's it, baby. Hold me and come with me. It's all yours, anything you want."

She burrowed deeper into him and clung with her arms and legs as he drew her to a final sweet burst of fulfillment that left them both replete and complete in each other.

Afterwards, he wrapped her in his arms and held her close. Before she drifted into sleep, he kissed her swollen lips once more and told her softly, "I love you, Anna."

As he tucked the quilt around them, she slept, limbs entwined with his in a lover's tangle.

Chapter Nine

"Sweetheart. Open your eyes."

The low, teasing voice reached through the haze of sleep and roused her.

"Come on, Anna. Please."

That was better. Let him beg, for a change. If he wouldn't let her sleep, that was the least he could do. She stretched slowly and became aware of his long, warm body wrapped around hers. His hands were smoothing her wild tangle of hair and exploring the lines of her face.

"Please, baby, wake up," he coaxed as he leaned down to kiss her eyelids.

"Why? Do you want to hear me beg some more?" Her voice told him she was thoroughly disgruntled and far from happy with him.

"Are you always cranky when you wake up?"

"Do you always wake up anyone you see peacefully sleeping?"

Jay drew her on top of him in a sleepy heap and arranged her sprawling long limbs comfortably. "Are you sulking?"

"Yes."

"Would it help if I let you tie me up and make me beg?" he asking teasingly. "I'm an equal opportunity lover."

That had possibilities. Anna considered some of them while he situated her more conveniently and let her know unmistakably why he'd woken her up. He wanted more. He really could go all night, she realized slowly. Her interest was engaged, if only to ponder the possibilities as an intellectual exercise.

Did she want to tie him up? Yes, but not yet. For now, she kind of liked the way he took charge sexually. He tied her up and it turned her on. He groped her in public and she was ready to come instantly. He made her beg for his cock and when he finally gave it to her, the orgasm was even more intense from the frustration and anticipation.

Jay didn't make her feel awkward or nervous about her inexperience. He just made her feel hot. He made her feel like a slut who would do anything as long as he pleasured Pavlov's pussy again and if she was honest with herself she had to acknowledge that she enjoyed the feeling.

She was going to take a turn dominating him sexually in the near future, however. When she'd gotten up to speed and felt confident enough to take the lead. Say in another week. That seemed only fair. But if she demanded everything he had to give and got it, then where would that leave them? She wasn't sure she was ready to find out.

"Anna, my beautiful angel. I want you. I want you so much it hurts. Wake up and love me again," he urged huskily, trailing heated kisses along the curve of her throat.

It amazed her but feeling the evidence of his desire and hearing it in his voice was enough to send heat curling through her in response. Being lusted after was definitely a heady experience. It made her feel sexy, desirable, eminently worthy of lust.

She stretched against him again, sliding over him, and smiled when he groaned in response. His arousal sparked hers further and kindled an answering fire. She rubbed against him again in a sensuous slither and sighed in delight at the feel of him. She loved it. She wanted more. She was addicted to his body. She just going to have to accept it—she was his and he could do anything he wanted with her. It wasn't like he was abusing the privilege. It was just hard to acknowledge that another person had so much power over her, that Jay occupied such a vitally important place in her life. It was hard to make the mental transition.

"Maybe I will," she muttered, torn between irritation at having begged for his body and interest in enjoying it again. Besides, her body wasn't having any trouble at all making the transition to full surrender. Maybe if she just followed her body, her brain would catch up.

"Love me?" Jay asked hopefully.

"Tie you up and make you beg," she clarified.

Jay lifted her chin and smiled at her. "Fine with me. I'll take what I can get." Then he turned serious. "I didn't do it to upset you. I wanted to make it better for you. If you didn't like it, I won't do it again."

Well, that was fair enough. Anna considered him just as seriously for a moment before practicing some more in-depth communication. "I liked it but I don't like not being in control," she informed him bluntly.

"I know." He moved upright to sit against the headboard and took her with him, keeping her in his lap with her legs tangled around him. "I wanted you to know that you didn't always have to be."

Philosophy, from her villain. What next? Anna didn't try to hide her surprise. "What do you mean by that?"

"I mean that you're a very strong woman. I wanted you to know that I'm strong enough for you to lean on. You can let me be in control if you want to or need to. I can take it," he explained sincerely. He smoothed her long hair back and continued thoughtfully, "You've never depended on anyone, have you? You're always in control."

Genuinely surprised, Anna thought that one over. Was she a little bit of a control freak? Maybe. She had the kind of job where she controlled all kinds of things. Harnessed the elements and bent them to her will. She controlled chemical reactions, carefully directed them to explode in a gradual release while producing the visual and auditory effects she designed.

On top of that, she was basically her own boss. Lyle gave her free rein to do just about anything she wanted to. She lived alone without even a pet to be answerable to. Maybe he did have a point.

"I never thought about it, Jay," she answered honestly. "I just did what I had to do. I had to take care of myself early on and maybe I just got used to being in charge."

"What about your family?" His voice told her he was genuinely interested, curious but not trying to push her.

Anna curled around him and snuggled closer while she thought about how to answer. It struck her as odd and yet somehow as natural as anything else about their relationship that they were discussing philosophy and her childhood while naked, aroused and inches from being actively sexually engaged.

"We weren't very close," she admitted. "I'm not sure they planned on me or knew what to do with me. I was an only child and my parents were very involved with their own lives."

Jay tucked her closer to his chest and stroked her bare skin in small, slow circles. "Uh-huh. So you got to be in control."

"Is that what this conversation is about?"

"In a way."

"Hmm. I'm beginning to think it wasn't just a whim that made you decide to tie me up the first time." She raked his shoulder with her teeth as if to teasingly punish him for premeditation.

"You'd be right," he admitted freely and gave her a love bite of his own.

"And why would that be?" Anna prompted, nipping at his throat.

"You haven't figured it out yet? Some brain you are," he chided and turned his head obligingly for her nibbles.

"Control?" She let her mouth explore the curve of his neck and the hollow spot behind his ear while her hands wandered over his back and up into his hair.

He groaned in pleasure. "I love that." His body told her the same thing as he reacted measurably to her teasing, his erection growing even harder. "No, wench. Trust."

"Trust. Explain, please."

He caught her hands and held them still while he kissed her. "I'm proving to you that you can trust me.

You're safe with me. You can scream, cry and lose control."

"Sounds kinky," she informed him archly.

"Kinky does not begin to describe it." He wickedly caught her ear and whispered something that made her shiver.

"Wow," she commented. "Is that possible?"

"Anything is possible, my love," he assured her. "I'm a determined man. I want to be involved in your life."

Anna laughed and slanted him a sardonic look. "I think you already are."

"Am I?"

Suddenly, he looked worried. Tall, dark and nervous. Very interesting look for a villain. But she didn't want him worried, for some reason she refused to examine.

"Yes, you are," she assured him firmly.

He didn't look convinced. "Do you think you can lean on me? Let me be the strong one, at least on alternate days? Or will you shut me out when you need me?"

Now she was really startled. "Do I shut you out?"

"Yes. You're a very prickly flower of passion. But I'm determined to get your blossom," he growled in mock ferocity and nuzzled her neck.

"Have you forgotten already? You did, ah, deflower me," she informed him modestly.

"Yes, and it was fun, too. Worth the thorns. Good thing you had them, or someone else might have done it," he mused out loud.

It was impossible to imagine that, Anna realized.

She kissed him sweetly. "My flower is all yours. And I think it needs some attention." She sat up straight and met his eyes. "You know, I've never done this before."

He nodded. "We just established that," he pointed out.

She lightly nipped at his lower lip in retribution. "I mean the trust part. I don't know the rules. You've done this and I haven't. I don't know what to expect or what you feel or what it means."

As a matter of fact, he hadn't done this before but he didn't think he'd tell her that yet. It just might scare her off. Trust was growing but it was still fragile. She really didn't understand, but she was his love. She held his heart and he'd never given it before.

If she knew, she might panic and drop it.

"We make the rules," he informed her solemnly. One thumb moved over her lower lip in a thoughtful caress. "We make choices and decisions based on what we both need and want. I want more than your wonderful body. Are you willing to give me more?"

So he hadn't been kidding about his kinky desires. He wanted inside her mind. Inside her skin. Anna studied him and tried to sort it out. "Jay, I'm not sure what you want from me."

He smiled at her. "I'm asking you to explore this with me, that's all. Explore what you need. What you want. Keep an open mind."

She laughed at that favorite platitude of his.

"I'm asking for intimacy," he informed her.

Now that was suspicious, considering. "If we were any more intimate right now, we couldn't talk," she pointed out.

Jay's smile widened. He shifted her, slid inside her and then they were as intimate physically as it was possible to get. "Like that, you mean?"

She sighed blissfully and dropped down against his chest. "I think you've created an insatiable monster," she informed him soberly as she tightened her legs around his waist.

"I'm not afraid," he assured her with a wicked look.

"I am. What if I collapse first?"

"I'll let you sleep through the rest," he offered generously. He moved her in a gentle rocking motion.

She laughed, a sound like rippling honey and Jay hugged her closer. "I love the way you sound," he told her. "And the way you feel. And I love being your only lover."

"I get the feeling you love to talk. Should I talk dirty to you?" Anna inquired innocently.

"Yes. Talk to me. Tell me what you feel, what you like." He kissed her forehead, cheeks and chin in a wonderful contrast to what his raging passion was doing elsewhere. That was Jay, hot animal sex and tender kisses.

"I like the way you look," she began seriously. "I like the way your body is shaped. I like the way you look so dark and forbidding outside but inside you're so playful and funny." She smiled at him. "You're an otter in bear's clothing."

Jay gripped her hips and moved her in a deep circle. "At least I make you think of an animal," he growled.

She laughed at his response. Then sobered. "Is it supposed to be like this? Is it okay to laugh in the middle?"

"It's okay to laugh as long as you don't laugh at my masculine size," he assured her. "We men are somewhat sensitive about that."

"Really?" She moved experimentally against him. "Why? I'd be more likely to scream than laugh. You're too big. I still don't know how this is even possible."

"Honey…" At her words, he felt himself get impossibly bigger. "You think that?"

"Of course I do."

He groaned and held her still while he fought for any little shred of control. "I like hearing you say that."

She caught on slowly but she did catch on. She gave him a wicked look. "You do?"

"I do. Tell me again."

"Tell you you're too big?"

He groaned feelingly. "Yes. Tell me I'm a monster and my cock is terrifying. Women would run screaming from the sight."

She almost had. She was deeply glad she hadn't. "Oh, Jay," she sighed. And proceeded to drive him over the edge and into the abyss with inventive and vivid naughty nothings whispered in his ear.

She asked him to fuck her with his big, hard cock and he carried out her request. She used words and combinations she'd never imagined she could say out loud. Jay acted as if everything she said and did was just exactly right and all of it turned him on. When she whispered, "My pussy is yours, Jay, take it," he started thrusting into her with a wild frenzy that had them both coming within seconds.

Afterwards, she was still grinning broadly. She hadn't been so far off, in the beginning, thinking he wanted to be talked to the peak. He really, really liked it.

"What's so funny?" Jay asked, stroking the curve of her jaw.

"I didn't have to tie you up to make you beg," she answered with clear satisfaction.

He kissed her sweetly. "Nope. I told you I'm an equal opportunity lover. Feel free to practice your wonderful communication skills on me anytime."

Anna kissed him back and settled into his embrace with a contented sigh. "I do need practice. I'm not always very good with words."

He hugged her tighter. "Oh, honey, believe me. You have a gift with words."

She responded in kind and hugged him back, then let her hands wander over him. "It seems I do," she sighed. "What do you know."

They cuddled for a while in silence, just enjoying the closeness. Finally Jay asked lazily, "Are you hungry?"

"Jay, I'm worn out," Anna protested with a groan. "I can't believe you aren't. You're not human. How about if I just talk some more?"

"Angel, angel. I meant for food." He grinned wickedly at her assumption and she blushed.

"Oh."

"Yes, 'oh'," he teased. "Want some dinner? A midnight snack? Anything?"

"If you're offering to feed me, I'm accepting. Just as soon as I can walk again," she answered sleepily.

"No problem, I can carry you," he assured her, then suited actions to words. He scooped her up, quilt and all.

"Aren't I too heavy for you?" Privately, she thought he'd been hauling her around enough to cause a slipped disc. It wasn't as if she was petite. Not that she didn't enjoy it.

He gave her a lust-filled look. "Not at all. You're no lightweight but I'm man enough for you, sweetheart," he teased and kissed the tip of her nose.

Jay tucked the quilt closer around her and continued to the kitchen, where he settled her on a chair before he rummaged through the refrigerator.

"Enough with the stupid names," she grumbled as she watched.

"But, baby, I explained," he protested. He poked his head over the open door to direct an innocent look her way. "It's a way of showing affection. You need a lot of affection."

"I do?"

Her doubtful voice made him smile.

"You do, cuddles," he assured her, his voice muffled by the door. "You've had a very affection-deprived life. I'm making up for it." He turned and shut the door, then stacked his booty on the counter.

Anna watched as he arranged cheese, crackers, cold cuts and veggie sticks and thought about that remark. Maybe he did have a point. Did she dislike nicknames or was she just not used to them? Eventually she decided they were kind of nice. He used nice words, like baby, cuddles, angel, sweetheart. He made her sound feminine and cherished. What did it hurt? She might as well give her approval, since she couldn't stop him.

"Okay. You can use pet names," she announced magnanimously.

"Glad you agree, doll." His laughing eyes gave away his mock-serious expression.

They shared the quilt, moving to the floor since they couldn't fit in the same chair, and munched companionably. It was nice, talking and cuddling and feeding each other bites, Anna decided. She wouldn't have thought of it. She was distinctly glad that Jay had.

When they finished, he wrapped his arm and some quilt around her to keep her warm and they walked back to bed together.

Anna curled into him readily when he laid down and reached for her. She'd missed a lot, sleeping alone. Something else she was glad to change. Jay was a warm, comforting presence in bed beside her. Like a life-sized teddy bear. Cuddly. Only unlike a bear, he cuddled back, tucked blankets around her and teased her mercilessly about hogging the pillows.

Funny how she hadn't even known what she was missing until he became her lover. "Comfortable?" Jay asked, nuzzling her cheek.

She nodded.

He kissed the top of her head. "Then go to sleep, love."

She did, with his legs tangled through hers and his hands cupping one hip and one round breast in a warm, sweet hold.

"My lover." She whispered the phrase out loud, testing it as she slipped into sleep.

She didn't hear him answer, "Yes, love. Forever."

Something was tickling her nose. Anna frowned and twitched away, burying her face protectively.

Something turned out to be Jay's lips. Undeterred, they continued to feather her with kisses.

She sighed and blinked groggily. "Are you always so lively when you wake up?" Anna asked bluntly.

"You make me feel lively." Warmth sparkled in his eyes as he smiled at her. "Sort of tingly all over. How about you?"

"You make me feel something, all right," she muttered and closed her eyes again.

"Oh? Tell me more," he suggested, intrigued.

"I don't know," she moaned. "I get this irresistible urge to do something like…" she let her voice trail off, then whacked him with a pillow. "Like that," she concluded in satisfaction.

"Baby." Heat deepened in his voice. "I love it when you play rough."

She kicked him lightly and then regretted it when he told her how much he liked that, too. Nothing discouraged him, she thought sourly. She might as well wake up and be annoyingly perky, too. If she could.

The downside to this new arrangement was a real problem with sleep deprivation.

"Honey, it's time to get up. I wouldn't want you to refuse to sleep with me tonight because I made you late for the first time in three years," he informed her.

She stretched and started to come alive. "Am I sleeping with you tonight?"

"Yes. Absolutely. Definitely. I forgot to tell you this rule? Lovers sleep together. It's a law," Jay informed her in an officious tone of voice.

"A law?"

"Yes, a little-known law, but still enforced. You have to sleep with me."

Anna laughed and rolled over him to stand up. "Clown. Let's get going, then, I wouldn't want you to be late either."

She padded off to the shower and turned it on, reflecting that she felt oddly at home instead of awkwardly out of place there. It just went to prove that her own home was in truly desperate need of decoration to rescue it from anonymity and bland obscurity. She found it hard to believe that it hadn't occurred to her sooner, that she'd been content to simply drift and live in an anonymous void. Maybe she hadn't been as soundly in control all this time as she'd thought.

Just maybe she was more in control now than she'd ever been, by taking risks and letting go. Whatever the case, Anna had to admit that she was happy, relaxed and even making a real breakthrough at work as a result.

Maybe her recent decisions, including playing with one mouthy lover, were finally providing her with real control.

Jay was continually surprising her, proving to be a person she could trust in spite of her initial impressions. He showed real concern for her well-being. He wanted to draw her out of her comfort zone without pushing her to do anything she wasn't comfortable with. A real contradiction in terms. But then, he was a bundle of contradictions. A bad boy on the outside. A marshmallow on the inside.

Her marshmallow intruded on her thoughts by joining her under the spray and Anna decided to be nice and wash his back. That led to laughter and more affectionate pet names, which she was starting to get used to and even look forward to.

"So when do we get to use the canoe?" Anna asked Jay while he handed her a towel afterwards.

"Ah-ha! I knew you wouldn't be able to resist the siren lure of white water and danger," Jay stated, shooting her a triumphant look that stated plainly that he'd known all along that he was right about her and canoes. "The answer to your question, angel, is whenever it's safe. Right now ice is melting and breaking up and the water's high. Give it a little bit longer. We'll be out perfecting our strokes and doing expert portages in no time," he promised.

"You should have let me buy you a wetsuit at the same time, though. You're going to wish you had one the first time you get dunked in a river," Jay added as he handed her the brush and gestured for her to precede him through the door.

"Portages?" Ann turned back with a questioning look.

"Sometimes a river trip has nasty rapids and we'll have to get out and carry the canoe past," he explained. "Miss one, and you'll be getting more danger than I care to expose you to. I can just imagine what Lyle would say to me if I lost you on a rock somewhere."

Jay shuddered theatrically at the thought of facing the in-depth lecture sure to follow such an event.

"I should have known. You wanted someone to help you heft the thing, didn't you?" Anna accused. Having hefted it onto the top of his car with him, she could testify that it was a sound reason to lure another person into canoe mania.

He gave her a ridiculously wounded look. "Hey, I'm not afraid of a little fast water. Or really big, sharp rocks, or steep, steep drops. I just wouldn't feel right about risking your lovely neck. And since it's your neck, certainly you should help carry the canoe in the spirit of good sportsmanship." Jay declared self-righteously.

"Uh-huh," Anna agreed sarcastically. "Like I said. All this talk of thrills and wild excitement is just the bait to hook yourself a porter."

"That's portager," Jay corrected and ruffled her long hair. Then he held up two ties. "Which one of these do you like best?"

"The longer, wider one. I could use it to gag you with."

"No, really."

Really, Anna thought snidely. Then she turned to a different track as she considered the erotic possibilities. Hmm. Maybe, someday.

She studied his color choices in the meantime. One in pale yellow sported a thin red stripe. The other, a vivid green, was splashed with a swirl of color shaped somewhat like a floral design.

"The green one," she decided. "Are those supposed to be flowers?"

"No. Real men don't wear flowered ties. They're supposed to suggest a floral theme without actually crossing the line to femininity," Jay explained.

He flipped the tie under his collar and tied it expertly. "This says I'm a sensitive guy, in touch with my softer side, but not the kind of guy you wouldn't want to go canoeing with."

He swept her off her feet to explain, mock seriously, "I'm a manly man. But sensitive." Then he kissed her quickly and set her back on her feet.

"You're a man in need of a gag," Anna remarked acidly. But she kissed him back.

"What's my lovely mad scientist going to be up to today?" Jay inquired casually as he leaned against the wall and watched her finish dressing. She was something, in any state of dress or undress. He was eagerly looking forward to many more viewing opportunities.

Anna smiled widely, her face alive with pleasurable anticipation and satisfaction. "Today, I light off the test Freedom Finale," she announced. Then she frowned. "And pray it works."

Curiouser and curiouser, thought Jay. "What if it doesn't work?" He was enjoying her enthusiasm for her work and he thought her little frowns of concentration were particularly adorable.

"Worst case? A total dud. Or a chain reaction instead of guided expulsion." At his blank look she explained further, "In other words, instead of a nice, steady burn resulting in a nice, steady launch with a controlled explosion at a safe height, it'll go off all at once on the ground or not far enough up."

Explode on the ground. Suddenly, she didn't look so adorable. Jay had a nightmare mental image of her broken, bloody body lying next to a large crater. "Just how likely is that?"

Anna looked up in surprise at his demanding tone. He was really nervous, she realized. She smoothed his tie and smiled reassuringly. "Don't worry. I'm a professional. I did preliminary tests and we practice all kinds of safety measures."

He didn't look convinced. He looked distinctly worried. Sweet of him, Anna thought. "Really," she promised.

He frowned at her. "Anna, if you blow yourself up I'm going to be very angry with you."

"Jay, statistically I'm in more danger in the shower," she pointed out.

"So we'll stop showering."

She had to laugh at his grim expression. "Keep an open mind," she teased, tossing his favorite phrase back at him. "Try to maintain a positive attitude. The danger's relative. I know what I'm doing and I'm very, very careful. I don't leave things to chance."

Jay continued to frown darkly at her. She hugged him. Why not? A little display of affection comforted her, so it should be good for him, too. At least it might distract him.

"Just be sure you are careful," he finally grumbled. "I'll sit on you while Lyle gives you a good talking-to if you aren't."

"You'll have to find the pieces first," she kidded and instantly regretted it when he turned white. She'd forgotten but some people were really nervous around explosives. To her, they were just the tools of the trade but it wasn't an uncommon phobia. It seemed to be the kind of thing that either bothered somebody deeply or not at all. Jay was apparently the type who was bothered by it.

"Jay, I'll be all right."

"You'd better be all right," Jay muttered at last.

She grinned at his unusual loss of poise and kissed him to distract him. It worked so well, they were nearly late.

Jay left her at her lab door with a final dire warning to keep herself the way he liked her, in one piece.

She shoved him on his way in mock exasperation. "Enough. Quit. I'll be fine but you are in danger of being hit by something explosive," she threatened.

That sparked a glint of humor in his dark eyes. "I love it when you get explosive with me," he told her with a sensual leer.

"So look forward to it. Later," she hinted broadly. "I have work to do around here."

"I'm going, I'm going." Jay proved once again that he was a man of his word. He winked at her as he backed away, hands raised to ward off her attack. "I'll see you later, my lovely."

Dark brows waggled suggestively at her just before he vanished around the corner.

Chapter Ten

It was incredible, Anna thought, gazing in wonder at the brilliant colors streaming in sunbursts of scarlet, white and cerulean blue against the dim gray spring sky. A bold display of pyrotechnic artistry. An awesome example of the mysteries of chemistry, harnessed and channeled to produce her vision in the sky. It was so beautiful, she wanted to cry.

Instead, she turned to beam at Jane, who was whooping in triumph beside her.

"You did it!" she cheered. "Amazing! You're a true wizard. Look how long the blue streaks hang."

Anna hugged her assistant, laughing like a loon. "Isn't it great? I love it. It's wonderful."

"Great? Wonderful? Anna, you outdid yourself on this one. Let's pack up and you can go tell the good news to Grant," Jane urged. "He'll probably offer you a cigar to celebrate."

That wasn't funny. He'd rave and puff as enthusiastically as he lectured. But Anna felt ready for him. After practicing on the man who topped him for the title of Company Big Mouth all week, she felt ready for anything. Especially when the thrill of discovery and success accompanied the new gains in her communication and personal skills.

And this was a major success, getting the blend of colors to burst and fall in unison, with a boom thrown in for the thrill of it.

Well, maybe she did harbor a teeny, little fondness for big explosions. Certainly it seemed like a fitting tribute to her explosive personal life of late. The explosive new Anna and her explosive affair.

Excitement welled up and bubbled over. In a burst of happiness, Anna danced around Jane in a crazy circle. "I love it!" she announced. "And you're the greatest assistant anyone, anywhere ever had. We should celebrate."

The two women packed up safety equipment and headed the little jeep from the test site back to the office building, awash with satisfaction at their accomplishment.

"I should go tell Jay, too," Anna mused out loud. "You won't believe this but I think he was actually afraid I'd blow myself to bits. The thought of me working with matches and black powder made him really nervous."

Jane rolled her eyes at that statement. "Gee. Why would a little thing like that bother anybody?"

"I don't know," Anna answered, matching her mocking tone of voice and doing her best to look ingenuous.

Jane considered her for a moment. "You know, that's really sweet. He worries about you. He feeds you. I don't know if you even noticed but he came by at lunchtime and brought you a sandwich since you were too involved to tear yourself away."

Now that she thought about it, Anna did vaguely remember Jay appearing and pushing a sandwich into her hand. She frowned. "Did I remember to say 'thank you'?"

Jane shook her head in mock despair. "You're hopeless," she declared. "Put you in front of an interesting problem and you forget everything and everyone else around you. Just go tell Grant the news and then stop in to show your intended that you're still in one piece, okay?"

Anna stopped dead in her tracks, brought abruptly back to earth by those words. "My what?"

"Intended. Come on, you can't tell me you aren't serious about this guy. And we've already established that he's serious about you," Jane pointed out, planting her hands on her hips in preparation for a confrontation.

Serious. The word echoed in Anna's head. Serious. Was she serious? What were her intentions? What were his? She honestly didn't know. The confusion showed clearly on her face and Jane made an exasperated sound.

"Which word didn't you understand?"

Anna eyed the tapping foot and flashing eyes in trepidation. She was in trouble now. Lyle's lecture would pale into insignificance compared to whatever Jane was about to throw at her. "All of them?" She attempted levity.

"Oh, boy. Can you say 'denial'? I knew you could," Jane smirked.

"I'm not in denial."

"Oh, sure. The man buys you a canoe and you're still not willing to face facts," Jane said.

"Let's just leave the canoe out of this," Anna muttered. No matter how much fun it was, no matter how many thrills it provided, she was beginning to think that canoe wouldn't be worth the amount of trouble it had already caused her.

Maybe what she really needed to do was to have a little confrontation with a certain canoeist and find out what he meant by wanting intimacy and more than her body. Explore her needs and wants… Exactly what did that mean, anyway?

Anna pushed aside the questions for the moment. Right now she had good news. No, make that great news. And to top it all, she also had some new ideas about an alternative to black powder that just might turn out to be the legendary and long-lost Greek Fire.

"I don't want to talk about it," she told Jane. "Right now I just want to go gloat to Grant and maybe give him an exploding cigar."

"And you'll talk to Jay?" Jane hinted broadly.

"I'll talk to him, I'll talk to him," Anna sighed, throwing up her hands in a mock plea for mercy. "I'll go show him personally that I'm still alive. I'll even remember to thank him for feeding me. And I'm going now!" she finished as she retreated hastily toward the stairs. She felt too good to wait for the elevator.

She turned and raced up the stairs, two at a time, her long braid flying behind her like a fiery whip. When she burst into Lyle's office, beaming and glowing with excitement, he actually dropped his cigar. Fortunately, it landed in the overflowing ashtray.

"Lyle, the Freedom Finale is ready!" Anna announced triumphantly. She then jumped onto the man's broad lap and planted an impulsive kiss on his weather-beaten cheek. "Isn't it great? Congratulate me!"

As the shock wore off, he did. The fatherly man hugged her and actually patted her on the head but Anna decided to let it slide. He was entitled. For all his bullheadedness and lecturing, he was a dear.

"Well. Well, now," Lyle boomed, getting slowly up to speed. "You've finished your new design, eh? That's my girl. I knew you'd do it. Well, well." He smiled, a gesture that threatened to crack his face and groped for his beloved cigar.

Anna laughed and hugged him back before jumping up to dance around his desk.

"Thank you for your vote of confidence. It's the most beautiful shade of blue and the bursts time out perfectly. It's great, Lyle."

"Good work, girl. I'm proud of you, damned proud," Lyle ground out. "Now, get yourself out of here and go celebrate your victory. Take that sorry new marketer with you, too." He jabbed at her with his cigar for emphasis.

"What, Jay?" Anna asked, startled.

"Not what, who," he corrected gruffly.

"Oh. You knew Jay and I were seeing each other?" Her surprise was evident.

"Ha. You think I don't pay attention to what's going on around here? You think I don't have my thumb on this company's pulse? What the hell do you think it is that I do, anyway, that's what I'd like to know."

He was winding up for a lecture, Anna realized in horror. She'd started him off. She'd better escape, and fast, or she'd be there until the lack of oxygen forced her to the floor in an effort to get below the smoke level.

"Fine, I'll take him," she promised so quickly that the words ran together as she backpedaled at top speed toward the door.

"You do that. And don't you come back here before Monday, you hear me? What you want to work weekends for, I don't know. You just—"

"Yes, sir, we're going, thank you, sir!" Anna cut him off in desperation then dashed out the door and slammed it behind her. She leaned against it, panting. A very narrow escape.

Once she'd recovered, she headed to Jay's office. Now that she thought about it, she hadn't gone to see him there once. He'd always come to her. Maybe that was what he'd meant, in part, at least. That he wanted her to meet him on his ground once in a while. Not a bad idea, either. She'd see a different side of him that way. And maybe he deserved to finally see some reciprocation, too. Things had been pretty one-sided so far.

When she reached Jay's office, he was on the phone but he waved at her to come in and indicated a seat at the sight of her in his doorway. Anna grinned at him in response to his welcoming wink and poked around while he finished. Even his office had personality, she noted with approval. Pictures, cards, a plant. Not the standard office rubber tree, either, but a sprawling philodendron.

She picked up a birthday card and read it with interest. She realized she didn't know when his birthday had been. She wanted to know. The comical card, making the typical getting older wisecracks, was from somebody named Michael. It occurred to her that she didn't know who his friends were or what Jay liked to do besides canoe and sleep with her. There were obviously many unexplored sides to him.

And suddenly Anna found herself wanting to explore them all. She wanted to know what Jay's childhood had been like, now that she'd told him about hers. What his family was like, if they were close. She'd never asked.

She'd been distracted by her desire to experiment with his incredible body and then she'd been further distracted by the discovery that the experiment changed everything. Her mind was still coming to terms with what her body had long since acknowledged and it had kept her from moving past being stunned to thinking about the future.

Her future included Jay. No more denial.

"Sweetheart!" Jay hung up the phone and came around to hold her. "Are you still in one piece?" He gave her a suspicious look and used the excuse to allow his hands to roam freely over her.

"Yes." Now that she was there, she didn't know what to say, so she just stared at him like a tongue-tied idiot.

"Yes, I guess you are," he agreed. His exploration verified that all her parts were where he'd last seen them. "Baby, you know how to make a man sweat," Jay concluded as he gathered her close.

Yes, she'd made him sweat, Anna silently agreed. But she wasn't going to do it anymore. She was going to learn how to be intimate and not shut him out. She could do it. She'd learned about communication, hadn't she? She could learn about intimacy, too.

She tentatively wrapped her arms around his waist and leaned against him. Where did she start?

Somewhere. Anywhere. She took a breath and asked, "Jay, are you busy?"

"Not really, love. I've got most of my business wrapped up for the day. Why?"

She met his eyes squarely, loving the fact that she could look him easily in the eye. "I finished testing the new Freedom Finale and it's done. Lyle gave me strict orders to get out and not come back before Monday and to take you with me." Her voice dropped dramatically. "I don't have to tell you what will happen if I fail, do I? I'll get lectured, Jay."

"Oh. I see. Well, we can't have that," Jay responded with mock seriousness.

"Thank you," Anna replied humbly. "I can't tell you what it means to me that you're willing to make a sacrifice like this for me. I mean, go off and spend the weekend with me, teaching me how to be your dream lover. I know I'm not very good at this yet. I need lots of practice." Her sultry voice got stunning results, Anna noticed happily.

"Tell me more," Jay breathed, his black eyes glistening with desire.

"Oh. Well, there's so much," she murmured throatily. "So much of you and I know so little. I'm afraid we'd better go right now and get started." Wicked delight glimmered in her violet eyes.

Jay gave a little groan and swung her around in a circle. "You bet, love. Anything you want."

She pushed against his chest at that, demanding his attention. "No. Wrong. I think it's about time you got everything you want," she promised seductively. For good measure, she blew in his ear and then nibbled at the sensitive cord of his neck.

"I'm all yours," he volunteered readily. "Make me your learning toy."

Anna gave him a hot, sweet kiss for a start. It was the least she could do in return for his generous tutoring in the wonderful art of French kissing.

When she let him up for air, she gripped his tie and held his eyes with determination. "No, you're not a toy. You're a man. A manly man, but one who's sensitive and in touch with his softer side." She waved the tip of his tie as a reminder.

"Come on, manly man. Let's go play." Anna beamed at him and tugged impatiently at the printed silk.

Jay followed, looking dazed and confused but very, very interested.

"Where do you want to go, precious?" he asked as he pulled her to his side in a possessive hold with one long arm.

"I want to go where you want to go," Anna answered promptly. "Jay, I've been selfish and mean. It's your turn. What do you want to do?"

"Why don't we get dressed up and go out for dinner?" Jay suggested. "We'll eat, talk and dance. Sound good?"

"That sounds wonderful," she answered dreamily. "I like dancing with you. Even when you're being obnoxious. And I want to talk to you, too. I told you about my childhood last night and I still don't know the first thing about yours." Anna gave him a serious look. "I think you were right about intimacy. I want to be intimate with you."

Jay wanted to be intimate with her, too. Badly. Painfully. Immediately. He didn't know what it was about her but he wanted her with an urgency he didn't understand. No matter how many times he took her, he wanted more. He hungered for her and he didn't think a lifetime would be long enough to satisfy all the needs she awoke in him.

"Me too, angel," he vowed. "Me, too."

Her smile widened at her response. He felt like he was looking into the sun. She was all fire and heat. She warmed his heart and his blood and ignited his soul.

"Good." Anna gave him an affectionate squeeze.

At the parking lot, she turned in his arms and kissed him again. "I think it's about time I took my poor car home," she informed him solemnly, violet eyes dancing. "People might talk."

"They might," Jay agreed.

They grinned at each other.

"I'll follow you back to your place then and we'll go to mine afterwards, all right?" Jay asked.

Anna nodded and they separated to solve the car problem. It really was funny that she'd made such a fuss about a mud-free parking space in her snit over her wrecked Nikes and since then she'd only used it once. She couldn't help laughing at herself as she drove. And she couldn't help thinking that Jay had even managed to take her mind off of the mud.

He stayed behind her and waved and blew kisses at lights, as if he hated being separated, even by a car length, as much as she did. Jane had been right, as usual, Anna thought. She was in denial. She was serious about Jay and it was time to do something about it. This weekend.

He made his usual dramatic fuss when they arrived at her house, running over to help her out of her car. She laughed at his antics and enjoyed his arms around her waist as they walked to her door. She'd missed so much, all these years. So much solid human contact. So much fun. Jay was right. She'd been affection-deprived and he was making up for it. She even waited eagerly to hear his silly nicknames.

"Beautiful, I missed you," he breathed against her lips, as if he knew what she was waiting to hear.

"Handsome, I missed you, too," she replied in kind.

Inside, he followed her to her room and sprawled across her bed. "Do I get to watch you get ready for our date?" Jay inquired with obviously prurient interest.

Anna arched a brow at his request. "Why? Do you like to watch?" she asked with the same heavy innuendo he was so fond of using. He knew she meant more than watching a woman change clothes.

Jay's eyes glowed like ebony flames. "Anna. I like to watch you when I'm inside you. I like to watch your face when you cry out for me. I like to watch your body turn to molten gold in my arms and burn for me."

Anna swallowed, her mouth suddenly dry at his scorching words. She slowly undressed for him while his eyes simultaneously devoured and worshipped her.

She was an idiot, she realized. He'd told her from the beginning how he felt and he'd shown her every minute since. She hadn't known love when it hit her in the face. His feelings for her were written openly in his eyes and in his hands, gripping her coverlet in two taut fists.

He did love her. The realization thrilled and frightened her. But he was a man worth taking risks for and she was determined not to hold back any longer.

When she stood naked, she posed boldly and let him see everything he wanted to, nearly feeling the loving touch of his eyes on her skin.

"What do you want me to wear?" Anna finally asked, her honey voice darkened with emotion.

"Me." Jay stayed put, watching her with palpable intensity. "I want to be inside your skin and everywhere outside. I want to wrap you in myself and hold you in my heart forever."

Anna trembled. Love wasn't just a word or a game. It was a power, an elemental force every bit as dangerous as those she directed every day in her laboratory.

"But for now, passion flower, I want you to wear what you were wearing the first time I saw you," Jay finished softly. He relaxed his grip and gave her a tender smile, as if he knew his intensity unnerved her and he wanted to put her at ease.

She found the garments she'd worn that night and slowly, deliberately, aware of her audience with every cell of her being, she put on the silky thigh-high stockings, rolling them up her long legs. Then she stepped into her fragile heels and turned her back to Jay in a provocative stance.

"Are my stocking seams straight?"

"Yes," he answered in an uneven voice that told her how deeply her performance affected him.

Anna smiled at him over her shoulder, and slipped into the satin merry widow, tugging it into place and smoothing the fabric that threatened to spill her generous curves out over the top.

Straps fastened to the stockings and the round garters slid up to support the tops. A tiny scrap of red satin covered her like a fig leaf. Then she walked to the closet to get her dress. She turned back to face him and the flapper gown fell around her like a sigh. She reached back to close the zipper. Ready, she went to him and waited.

"Anna," he whispered. "Don't move. Don't say anything." While she stood like a statue, he raised one shaking hand to stroke the soft fabric from her hips to her ribs.

"Oh, honey. You are beautiful. I want to wait and if you move at all, I won't be able to." The fierce hunger in his eyes held her still and after a minute he stood beside her and drew her slowly against him.

His cheek rested against hers and their hands entwined. They swayed together as if they danced to some silent music. Finally, he tugged her toward the door in an unspoken command and she followed his lead willingly, still held in the thrall of his sensual spell.

He'd given himself to her unstintingly, over and over. Tonight, Anna vowed, she'd give herself to him just as completely. He deserved nothing less. He deserved the intimacy he'd asked for. He deserved to have his love cherished by the one he gave it to.

And it was easy to do. He'd shown her how.

Jay tucked her into his car with a final shivery caress along her jawline. Then he joined her on the other side and held her hand tightly while he drove. Anna didn't say anything. She didn't want to break the aura of anticipation and seduction.

He didn't speak either, until they reached his home. Then he only said, "Wait," before going around to open her door for her.

She let him help her out and walked beside him in a dreamy haze. Inside, he pushed her onto a chair and left her there while he dressed for her.

Secretly, Anna hoped he'd produce a tuxedo. He looked wonderful in all monochrome. Odd that such a Technicolor personality came packaged in natural black and white coloring. She wondered with unscientific whimsy if he'd developed such a colorful personality in reaction.

When he came back for her, smiling faintly and looking like a sardonic devil in black and white formal dress, he took her breath away.

How had she failed to notice that first night that he was possibly the most spectacularly handsome man she'd ever seen? How had she introduced herself to him without salivating on his cummerbund?

"I have something for you," he said and gestured for her to turn around. She did. Something turned out to be a brush. Jay unbraided her long hair and smoothed the freed mass in lazy, lingering strokes. Anna gave a blissful sigh and leaned against his legs while he brushed her hair.

"You have such beautiful hair," he informed her admiringly. "You look like a golden flame."

Then he fastened something cold around her neck.

Anna looked down and tried to see over his hands. Jay laughed at her frustrated curiosity.

"Come on, we'll go see it in a mirror," he told her and guided her over to one.

Jay stood behind her, his hands resting on her shoulders. Before him, Anna saw the same woman in the mirror she'd seen the first time she'd tried on the dress. Only now her confidence had an added element. A new light of emotion gleamed in her eyes and a new awareness softened her features. Love made her glow like the flame Jay likened her to, from the inside out. Behind her, his bold, dark good looks made the perfect foil for her fiery coloring.

As her eyes traveled downward, she saw it. A gold choker set with rubies circled her throat.

Anna caught her breath as she looked at the circles of fire that glowed against her white skin.

Jay's long fingers smoothed her throat and stroked the hollows of her shoulders. "Beautiful," he said with a smile to her reflection.

She smiled back, meeting his ebony eyes in the glass.

"You think so?"

"Oh, yes."

"You look pretty good yourself."

Jay preened modestly. "It's good of you to say so."

He knew very well he was the tall, dark and handsome type women dreamed about and Anna was sorely tempted to kick him for his smug attitude. But she decided to accept the bribe instead and continued to admire her rubies.

Chapter Eleven

"Why rubies?" Anna asked curiously on the way to the restaurant.

Jay sent her an incredulous look. "An unbelievably handsome and inventive lover, not to mention one blessed with an unusual capacity for endurance, gives you rubies and you want to know why?"

"I'm a scientist. It's my job. I ask why for a living," Anna reminded him with mock seriousness.

"Baby, I keep telling you, that's your problem. You ask too many questions. You think too much. Sometimes, you should just go, 'look at the pretty red things'."

"Hmm. How about, 'look, with these I can make a whopping beam of coherent light'?"

Jay shook his head in dismay. "Do I even want to know what coherent light is?"

"A laser. Rubies work really, really well."

Anna sounded a little too enthusiastic for his peace of mind and he shot her a threatening glance. "Don't you dare go and make some kind of high-tech toy out of that necklace. That's a piece of art, a work of beauty for my beauty, and if it comes off your lovely neck, I may have to wring it."

Anna gave a low, rippling laugh. He was so easy to tease. He really thought she'd cut up her necklace and use her rubies? He had to be out of his mind.

They were obviously the kind of gift a lover gave. They were an accolade to amorousness and Anna treasured them for the thought. He'd given her a salute to passion and that touched her far more than the monetary value. He'd called her his beauty and that was enough to make any right-thinking woman smile.

Anyway, she silently defended, if she was going to make a laser, she'd use industrial rubies, not true gems like the beauties winking around her throat.

But she let Jay think she might, since it made him so delightfully nervous.

"You certainly give unusual gifts," she mused out loud, taking another route since he hadn't answered her original question. "A canoe, with special paddles and life jackets. The most bizarre floral arrangement I've ever seen, with possibly the worst poem in the history of written language. And now a ruby choker. That's variety." Anna let her statement hang, inviting a reply.

"Variety is the spice of life," Jay returned blandly.

Anna waited.

"An unusual woman demands unusual presents," Jay finally informed her haughtily. "I match the present to the person. You, my dear, are an L.L. Bean canoe with accessories, loud and large floral arrangement, bad poetry, ruby choker kind of woman."

Well, that was a nice answer. Very nice. Anna liked it better the more she thought about it. So he appreciated many facets of her, just as she knew he wanted her to appreciate his many sides.

"It takes an unusual man to give unusual presents," Anna remarked, stroking his jacket sleeve and his ego simultaneously.

"Yes, it does," Jay agreed.

She regretted feeding his ego. Now she could practically feel it swelling and crowding her against the door.

He continued in the same vein, "Someday, precious, you'll come to appreciate all my unusual qualities. In the meantime, I want to hear you say 'look at the pretty red things', okay?"

Anna gave him a wide-eyed, innocent look and made an 'oh' shape with her lips. "Look at the pretty red things!"

"That's better." Jay patted her thigh approvingly. "Now say, 'Jay, how can I thank you?'"

Anna was happy to play along. "Jay, how can I thank you?"

"Oh, baby, I'll think of something." The heartfelt voice was accompanied by a blatant look down the neckline of her dress. Anna thought she could actually feel his eyes on her cleavage.

She didn't think she'd ever been happier.

"Jay, tell me something. If I put my foot in your lap and stroked you with my toes, would you like it?" she inquired thoughtfully.

The car swerved sharply and Jay made an abrupt correction.

"Honey." He sounded dazed again. "Yes. But don't you dare do it tonight at dinner or you'll ruin my plans."

Anna leaned her head against his shoulder and idly traced a pattern on the fabric covering his warm thigh. "You have plans for tonight?"

"I've been working on them all day," he answered smugly.

"All day?"

"Well, not all day. I had work to do, too. But I wanted tonight to be special, no matter what happened with your test, providing you lived through it. If it worked, you'd want to celebrate and if it didn't, you'd need some cheering up," Jay explained.

Anna was touched even more deeply by that statement. He'd thought about her feelings and was already prepared to comfort her if she had a disappointment.

"What were you going to do if it didn't work?" she asked curiously.

"Now, honey, do you think I'm going to tell you?" He gave her a sardonic look. "As brilliant as you are, everyone has a defeat once in a while. I stand ready to surprise you and cheer you up whenever it may happen to you."

"Hmm. Whenever is a long time," Anna mused, teasing him. "You really think planning on 'whenever' is a good idea?"

Jay teased her right back. "You aren't going to get your 'better luck next time' present, so give up."

"More presents?" Anna sat up and looked at him.

"Tonight, you only get the 'congratulations' presents," he said firmly.

He made her feel like a child, eagerly looking forward to whatever surprise he had planned. And at the same time he made her feel like a strong passionate woman, with the added thrill of knowing that he liked her that way. He admired who she was, not just what she looked like, though he was always quick to let her know he did appreciate her body.

He was some lover, Anna thought again, warmed all the way through with happy anticipation. She hugged her feelings for him to herself and thought that this must be what it felt like to fall in love.

Sort of tingly all over.

Anna remembered Jay's words and smiled inside.

It was nice to know that he was feeling tingly all over, too. And sometime during the weekend, she'd find the right time and the right way to tell him that she felt the same.

Too bad he hadn't taken her 'whenever' bait.

Or maybe he was skillfully avoiding the subject. She hadn't exactly given him any reason to think she was interested in making him a permanent fixture in her life. He'd told her he loved her and she'd said 'oh'. Then she'd tried to leave. And she hadn't mentioned it again.

Anna winced inwardly at the thought. She'd been so callous to his feelings. Suddenly she wondered why he didn't seem discouraged. He'd continued to tell her how he felt, pursued her relentlessly, asked for intimacy. Why hadn't he given up?

He'd also done a lot of planning ahead, she soon discovered. They had a reserved table for two in a quiet corner at the restaurant. A bucket of champagne waited for them and a single blue rose lay across one gilt show plate.

Anna picked it up and sniffed appreciatively. It had the rich perfume most hothouse flowers lacked and she fingered the velvet texture in admiration.

"Jay, this is beautiful. How did you get a blue rose?"

He looked secretive and smug, his black eyes gleaming at her in the low lighting. "I have a secret supply."

"Come on," Anna wheedled. "I really want to know."

He gave her a thoughtful look. "All right, beautiful. You haven't seen my garden yet, have you?"

She shook her head. They'd always been at his place at night, or in a hurry to get to work, or in a hurry to… She pulled her mind back to the present abruptly.

Too late, however. He'd already seen the blush staining her cheeks and she blushed redder when he just laughed and winked.

"Yeah, I haven't had a chance to give you a tour of the place yet, have I?" Jay teased her wickedly, enjoying her embarrassment. "Well, my best buddy Michael was in business college with me but he dropped out to be a carpenter. He's sort of a Zen master type and didn't like the corporate life. Anyway, he's really big on cultivating roses. He's the one who planned and planted my garden. He lives in New Hampshire, so I asked him to send me a blue rose."

Anna absorbed the information, fascinated. He had a best friend who grew roses? She would never have guessed that. And his friend had sent her the rose. What a nice man.

"But how did he get it blue?" she persisted.

Jay shrugged. "I think it's a special variety but maybe he used food coloring on it. I don't know. I didn't ask, honey. I just knew if anyone could come up with a blue rose, he could. Being that kind of friend, he didn't even ask why."

Anna batted her lashes flirtatiously at him. "You didn't tell him about me?" What she wouldn't give to have heard that conversation. Jane knew everything about their relationship, most of it before Anna did. How would things look to Jay's friend?

"No." Jay's unusually firm, serious tone took her by surprise.

"No?"

"No. Have some champagne." He busily poured for her and then was saved from more questions by the convenient arrival of their waiter.

Anna eyed him as he threw himself into ordering dinner and then sipping his champagne. Like a man trying to change or at least avoid the subject.

Then it occurred to her that he wouldn't be likely to tell his friends about her because he didn't know where he stood. She stroked the plush petals thoughtfully once more, then laid the rose down to pick up her flute and touch the rim to Jay's before they drank in unison.

"Thank you for the rose, however it got its color," Anna said with a smile. "And maybe I can thank your friend someday."

Jay looked distinctly uncomfortable and unsettled at that. "You're welcome," he finally answered. Then he straightened his tie and turned the conversation to her recent success.

She wasn't going to let him get away with it. She was going to get him to talk about himself, not spend the time they had talking about her life.

But it was just possible that in this particular case the best way to get what she wanted was to give him exactly what he asked for.

In depth. And detail. At length.

Anna grinned inwardly and proceeded to launch into a discussion of velocity stress, solid-propellant grains that did or did not retain structural integrity while burning, the fact that powdered titanium caused the familiar booming sound in fireworks while potassium benzoate caused the whistling sound and the various substances used for colors.

His wonderful eyes were glazing over beautifully when she wrapped up with a brief history of pyrotechnics.

"It was an old Chinese custom to light a firecracker in the morning to scare away evil spirits," Anna intoned in her best monotone lecture voice.

He'd finally had enough, she noted gleefully.

He roused himself from his stupor enough to interject a question. But unbelievably, he wanted to ask her about yet another work-related subject.

"What exactly is Greek Fire?"

Anna was amazed. He wasn't normal. His ears should be bleeding. His brain should be melting slush. He should be begging her to stop. He should be ready to sing like a canary and tell her everything she wanted to know about himself.

Anything to get off the subject.

And instead he wanted to hear about her pet project.

"Greek Fire," she repeated faintly. She gave him an odd look. "Nobody knows, that's the problem. We know it wasn't black powder, known more familiarly as gunpowder. It was something else and it was lost." She sipped her champagne with a distinct frown at the thought. "It's a mystery. That's the trouble with military secrets, the wrong people die, their side loses and their knowledge dies with them."

"Lyle tells me you're likely to rediscover it."

Anna smiled in mingled surprise and pleasure at that telling remark. "Lyle said that?"

Jay nodded. "He has great faith in your abilities."

Well, that was quite a vote of confidence. It warmed her. "It's a pet project of mine," Anna admitted. "I love a mystery and knowing it was discovered once, it has to be possible to stumble across it again. It has more possibilities than just military applications, you know. But Jay, why do you want to talk about all this?"

To her surprise, he suddenly looked a little hurt. Also a little angry. "I'm not too dumb to follow along, Anna. I can understand enough to get a rough idea of what it is that you do. You can talk to me about your work."

She stared back at him in silence, trying to sort that reaction out. "I didn't think you were, well—"

"Interested?" Suddenly his black eyes burned. "I'm interested in you. I care about whatever you're interested in."

He saw how much that impassioned outburst surprised her and he softened. Jay reached out to take her hand and twine his fingers through hers. "Honey, it doesn't bother me if you're the biggest brain of the century. We're different but it isn't a matter of better or worse. You're brilliant at what you do. I'm a whiz at marketing. And we'd both be serious failures if we traded jobs. You don't have to worry about me not being able to follow you, okay?"

Anna blinked back sudden tears. He was doing it again.

"You're doing it again," she informed him in frustration.

"Doing what?"

"Doing everything. Being nice, understanding, supportive. How am I supposed to meet you halfway if you insist on doing everything all the way?" she demanded.

Now it was Jay's turn to look surprised.

"I want to talk about you and you keep wanting to talk about me. All we've ever done is talk about me. I'm not completely selfish and uncaring, you know," Anna pointed out indignantly. "Just because you have all the experience at being a lover doesn't mean I can't learn. I'm not stupid either, you know."

Ebony eyes sparkled with humor. "Precious, are we having our first fight?"

Anna fought a smile in return. "I don't know. Don't the other three or four fights count?"

Jay gave her a sexy smile. "Nah, those were just little sparring matches. Warm-ups." He leaned back and lazily toyed with her feet under the table before sliding one foot suggestively up and down her calf. "Let's take this opportunity to further your communication skills. You seem a bit perturbed with me. Why?" In spite of his teasing look, his voice was serious.

Amethyst eyes darkened with ire. "That's a perfect example right there. Because you keep doing it all. I don't get a chance to do anything for you. Before I can, you're already pouring me champagne and playing footsies."

Jay eyed her in undisguised surprise. Just like that? She was ready to take the lead already? He hadn't even had time to romance her on the dance floor, feed her chocolate raspberry torte in between passionate kisses or bring her champagne and strawberries in bed. He'd planned to deposit the berries in convenient spots and nibble to both their hearts' content. In fact, he had a whole list of seductive plans to woo her with. And now, just like that, she wanted to turn the tables on him before he'd even gotten started?

He was even better than he'd thought.

The happy realization warmed him all the way through. Anna loved him and she was ready to demand that he do the right thing, any time now.

Damn, but he was amazing, Jay mused, congratulating himself with hidden glee. She'd be proposing to him in no time. Now he just had to let her seduce him.

"Sweetheart, I didn't mean to make you feel left out," he assured her. "I love meeting you anywhere. Halfway, all the way, anyway, as long as it ends up with you and me in the same place."

She blinked. "Oh."

Had any woman, anywhere, ever looked more adorable? Jay didn't think so. Love welled up in his heart until he could barely contain it.

He went on, "Honey, let me be romantic for you tonight." She'd be well and truly tied up in knots by the time he was done with her, he gloated. "I planned tonight. I was looking forward to it and I want to sweep you off your feet with blue roses, candlelight and dancing. Please?"

For good measure, he gave her his best melting look and hoped he wasn't too out of practice with it.

She looked suspicious. "You want to do all that?"

He loved her, he really did, Jay thought. He knew she was a big brain. But she really wasn't too bright sometimes.

"Yes, honey. I'm a manly man, remember? I love to make you swoon with passion, it makes me feel so powerful." He wiggled his brows at her suggestively and succeeded in making her laugh.

"Oh." Anna still looked adorably confused. "But when do I get to make you swoon?"

"We'll take turns," Jay assured her with dancing eyes. "It's my turn now and then it'll be your turn tomorrow. We have lots of time, right?"

Well, yes, they did, Anna conceded inwardly. But she was feeling distinctly impatient, wanting to get on with showing and telling him that she really did love him back.

Or was that exactly what he was asking for? He wanted her to let him take the lead. That could be part of leaning on him like he'd asked her to, couldn't it? A part of intimacy, letting him be involved in her life?

Yes, that had to be exactly what he was doing, Anna concluded. Talking to her about her work because he wanted to share what was important to her and wanted to be involved in what her life revolved around.

Had revolved around, she corrected herself sharply.

Now, her life revolved around something far more beautiful, more fascinating and complex, more dangerously explosive.

Love.

As a focus for life, it was much, much better than work and infinitely more satisfying.

She loved him. It was that simple. And if he wanted to make her swoon, then she'd swoon like no other woman ever before or since, Anna vowed. She'd be the swooningest lover in the history of the world. She'd follow his lead anyplace it went. And knowing his boundless enthusiasm for nocturnal gymnastics, she had a fair idea of just where it would lead. Something worth swooning over, she was pleasantly sure.

Maybe they could finally try some of those things with food. The whipped cream idea, for instance, she reflected in warm anticipation. And whatever they didn't get around to tonight, she'd make him swoon with tomorrow when it was her turn.

"Lead me," Anna invited Jay breathily and touched her champagne flute to his eagerly.

He looked distinctly pleased at her response. Good.

She'd get the hang of swooning in no time. She was a quick study.

It proved to be incredibly easy to do, too. He fed her bites from his plate, kept refilling her wine glass and giving her longing, lustful looks while he toyed with her deliciously under the table. Even a fool could learn to swoon with that kind of encouragement.

And she was no fool.

Dinner passed in a sensual haze of anticipation and delight. Anna savored every moment of his flair for romance that evidently matched his flair for drama.

For dessert, Jay fed her ripe strawberries dipped in dark chocolate. Between the hot looks he gave her, the rich flavors melting on her tongue and the wicked wanderings of his foot snuggled beneath the hem of her dress, Anna was thinking of going into swooning professionally.

"I think I've changed my mind," Jay informed her gravely as he watched her lick the last trace of chocolate from the corner of her mouth.

"Oh?"

"Yes." Heat and the promise of pleasure glittered in the depths of his ebony eyes. "I don't want to dance with you anywhere public. I want to take you home, light candles and put on some soft music. I want to feel you melting in my arms like warm honey. Then I want to undress you, piece by piece, until you're wearing nothing but the shoes and stockings you started out in."

Anna didn't have to work at swooning at all by the time he finished that stunning description. No wonder he liked naughty nothings. The explicit words packed an erotic punch that dazed her and sent a flood of heat to all his favorite erogenous zones in preparation for him to carry out the delicious threat. She felt flushed and tingling in mere anticipation of his private version of dirty dancing.

"What do you say, Anna?" Sensual promise made Jay's voice husky.

"Yes." Her normally smooth voice was uneven.

He rubbed one hard thumb over the velvet softness of her full lower lip. "You're going to say 'yes' again," he promised knowingly. "And again, and again. I'm going to love you tonight until you can't speak or breathe."

She couldn't speak now. She could hardly wait for the rest.

On the ride home, Jay slipped in a tape of sultry jazz and traced his way from the curve of her cheek to the shadowed valley above the plunging neckline with the soft petals of the rose.

The light, teasing caresses were a titillating prelude of things to come that sent shivers of delight down Anna's spine.

"Do you like that, sweetheart?" he asked, knowing the answer.

"Oh, yes," she responded with feeling.

The flower slowly trailed over the curves outlined in red satin, circling the peaks teasingly before gliding down to trace lazy patterns over her inner thighs.

"I'm going to touch you all over, just like this," he informed her in a voice dark with desire. "Soft and slow, until you can't take anymore."

Anna sighed mockingly. "Promises, promises."

Jay laughed at her impatience. "Just wait, sweet. I'll keep every promise and it'll be so good, you'll cry. You'll see stars. I don't have to be a rocket scientist to put you in orbit."

She believed him. He moved her to feel everything with an intensity she'd never imagined, to respond with a passion she didn't know she had and to want more.

Once they reached their destination, Jay led her by the hand to his den. Tall white candles gave away the fact that he was carrying out more of his planned seduction and had never intended to do anything else. The kind of dancing he preferred would have gotten them both arrested in any public place.

"Changed your mind, hmm?" Anna slanted him a teasing look from beneath thick lashes as he lit the candles with a ready taper.

He grinned back unabashedly. "I did tell you I'd planned this in advance," he reminded her.

"Yes, you did," she had to agree. It was still sneaky, however.

"But I have to admit that I didn't really know what you'd had on under that dress before." As the music started, Jay took her hands and drew her against his hard length. "If I had, you would never have escaped me that first night."

Anna flashed him a disdainful look. "I was armed. Well, heeled," she corrected. "What makes you think you could have stopped me from going anywhere?"

"This."

In explanation, he claimed her mouth in soft, clinging kisses.

"And this."

His hands ran over the delicate fabric in a feathery caress before closing over her rounded hips and pulling her against his thrusting member.

Heat settled in the pit of her stomach and she melted, molded herself against him, unconsciously seeking to get closer in response to his readiness, her hunger answering his.

Jay made a hoarse sound of encouragement against her lips and drew one hand up her side until it slipped between their torsos to cradle the aching weight of one full breast.

"Jay," Anna whispered. Her whole body responded to his touch. Waves of heat gathered wherever their bodies met. She could feel her breast swelling and hardening into his palm.

"More?" he asked, slipping the tip of his tongue along the corner of her mouth.

She nodded. In response, he cupped the sensitive undersides of both breasts and slowly rubbed the hardened tips with the pads of his thumbs. His erotic, rhythmic touch moved in time to the music and he used the sensual hold to lead her as they danced.

Warm kisses covered her lips and his tongue brushed lightly against hers in tiny strokes. When his hands came around to her back and pulled her more fully against him, she didn't register the zipper sliding down until her dress fell in a flaming puddle around her feet.

Jay lifted her clear of it, sliding her up his torso and then letting her slip back to the ground when her shoes were free of the entangling folds of fabric.

"I love this," he informed her with a low groan. "You, dressed like that, in those shoes. My Miss Firecracker."

The possessive note didn't grate on her. She liked the sound of it. She liked the pride he took in her beauty, the hunger in his eyes when he looked at her in the candlelight.

"Your skin glows like pearls against the fire in your hair," Jay continued. "And this makes you look wickedly wild." His hands roamed over the carnelian merry widow as he demonstrated his meaning.

"It makes me look like a very expensive plaything?" Anna couldn't resist teasing.

"Is that one of those trick questions that a smart man wouldn't answer?"

She gave him an innocent look then licked his lips in a tormenting caress. "Would I try to trip you up?"

He laughed softly then trapped her tongue with his for a moment before he answered. "In that case, angel, you should know you look like a woman any man would want anytime, anywhere, on any terms."

Now that was a good answer. She had to admit it excited her to think of herself as an irresistible object of desire. Maybe there was a fantasy there to play out with Jay sometime.

"And now I want you to take this off." Jay tugged at her thin ribbon straps demandingly then ran his fingers under the edge of the fabric to stroke her soft skin.

Anna smiled at him in answer and reached behind to unfasten the tight corset-style garment and let it slide down to reveal her full breasts by inches.

Jay reached for her as the merry widow fell to the floor and dragged her into his arms. The fabric of his jacket and the cold buttons on his dress shirt teased her bare skin in conflicting sensations.

He buried his face in her hair as they swayed together, their feet barely moving, the dance forgotten as they started an immeasurably older one.

"I want you," he whispered and Anna thrilled at the naked need in his urgent voice. "I want you, honey, so much that once I start I won't be able to stop."

"I don't want you to stop." Anna pressed closer to him and tilted her head to offer her mouth to his again.

"Oh, honey." Jay kissed her with a fierce desire in startling contrast to the soft persuasion he'd started with. Anna responded to the wild passion in his kiss, molding her body against his sinuously. She melted in his arms and offered herself to him to in total surrender.

"Anna." Her name was a raw whisper of sound. "Anna."

"Yes," she answered huskily.

He dragged her down to the floor, all patience gone. Buttons popped as he tore open his shirt and she helped him with hungry hands. She pushed back his jacket and ran her palms over the bare skin accessible under his dress shirt, needing to touch as desperately as she needed to feel him touching her.

Jay fumbled briefly with his pants, too far gone to bother undressing. He jerked them open, yanked the satin scrap separating them away and surged into her in one urgent thrust.

"Sweetheart," he managed to get out in a voice rough with passion. "I shouldn't be doing this to you. I still have my shoes on."

"So do I," Anna answered wickedly. She was certain a really bad girl wouldn't stop at a time like this to remove her shoes.

He gave a half-laugh, half-groan at her response.

"Jay, there's a time for romance but right now I don't want to wait anymore," she whispered. Then she kissed him until he quit fighting and gave them both what they needed.

In the glowing candlelight, they came together in a sudden firestorm that consumed them both and then left them to rest together in the embers.

Chapter Twelve

Jay propped himself up on one elbow and slowly traced the outline of Anna's face. She smiled and turned into his touch. Her eyes were still closed and he feathered a caress over her soft lashes, stroked the line of her nose and brushed the width of her velvet lips.

"Honey?"

"Mmm."

"I didn't hurt you, did I?"

The worry in his voice prodded her to open heavy eyelids and smile at him. "You could never hurt me," she assured him.

He smoothed a long strand of hair back from her forehead. "I should have at least taken my shoes off," he said with a frown. He ran his hands over her smooth legs as if to reassure himself that no bruises marked the white skin.

"Jay. I'm fine." Amusement and satiation glimmered in her jeweled eyes.

"No thanks to me." He gathered her up and cradled her against his chest as he carried her to bed. "Was the floor too hard?"

Anna groaned and leaned her head against his shoulder. "I can't believe you would worry about the floor at a time like this," she informed him. She wound her arms around his neck and snuggled closer.

Jay hugged her in response. "I won't do it again. I'll make sure that there's something soft in every room in case desire overtakes us again."

Anna laughed at that statement. "Not a bad idea, lover. I think the chance of desire overtaking us too far from the bed again in the near future is very good." She toyed absently with the remaining buttons on his shirt. "But you have to admit some things are worth a little sacrifice."

He settled her against the pillows and she propped herself up to watch as he finished undressing before he came back to remove her shoes and carefully roll down her stockings.

"I think I like this," she teased, arching her foot and raising her leg for him. "It's so much more fun when you take my clothing off me than when I put it on."

Jay gave her a thoughtful glance. "I don't know. I was having fun watching you put these on."

"Yes, I remember." She smiled in sweet satisfaction at the memory.

He dropped the filmy stockings by her shoes and joined her against the pillows. Anna took advantage of his nearness to nibble happily at his chin and lips.

"What are you doing, wench?" Jay yanked her on top of his sprawled form and cradled her head against his chest.

"Enjoying myself." The smug tone in her voice rang clearly and he found himself smiling slightly at it.

"Honey, I meant to go slower. I'm sorry." He kissed her forehead lightly and smoothed her long wavy hair down her bare back. "Next time, I'll make it better for you."

Anna laughed again at that statement. "Better than that? You've got to be kidding. If you do, I guess they'll say I died happy." She nuzzled his chin and cuddled closer.

"Don't try to make me feel better," Jay grumbled. "I was being romantic and I ended up throwing you on the floor and driving into you without even taking off my clothes."

"Well. If you hadn't gotten your pants unzipped, I admit it could have caused a problem," Anna agreed solemnly.

He considered that.

"You really didn't mind?"

"Oh. I get it. You want feedback." She settled herself more comfortably, draping one thigh over the outside of one of his and nestling her other knee in between his legs before she provided the praise he was waiting for.

"Jay, the candlelight was very romantic. The music was wonderful. You dance like Fred Astaire, only better, and I find it incredibly sexy that you were so overpowered by the sight of me in nothing but my stockings and high heels that you nearly did permanent damage to yourself before you got your pants open." Laughter lurked in her honeyed voice.

Jay rubbed his cheek against the softness of her hair. "Incredibly sexy, huh?"

"Uh-huh."

"You liked the music and the candles?"

"Very, very romantic," she assured him. "Soft and dreamy. Perfect."

"You think I dance like Fred Astaire?"

"Better."

While he thought that over, she added, "Besides, I don't know what you're worried about. It's not the first time we ended up on the floor."

"True." Jay kissed the top of her fiery curls. "But I wasn't setting out to romance you and sweep you off your feet at the time."

"I'd say throwing me to the floor in a fit of passion qualifies for sweeping me off my feet," she pointed out drowsily. "My feet were definitely pointed up in the air, not flat on the floor."

She did have a point there, he mused. That did qualify for being swept off her feet.

It just wasn't the way he'd wanted to do it.

"I wanted it to be really special. Like something out of a movie. Something like Rhett Butler carrying Scarlett up the stairs. Or James Bond."

She smiled against his bare skin. Only he would consider James Bond as romantic as Rhett and Scarlett on the staircase. "I'll take away your license to thrill. Will that make you feel better?"

She playfully nudged his calf with her toes and he responded by trapping her foot with both legs.

"No."

"Hmm. As the one who inflamed you beyond your ability to resist and ruined your plans, I feel a certain obligation to keep you from pouting," Anna murmured. "What would make you feel better?"

He toyed with her hair and said what he'd been wanting to say for days. "Move in with me."

She didn't answer immediately and his heart sank.

It was too soon. He'd pushed her before she was ready. And after he'd sworn he wouldn't make an issue of it.

"Let me guess," Anna said finally. "You had an ulterior motive for wanting to romance me and sweep me off my feet. You planned to ask me this after you had me properly swooning."

"That's it, honey," he agreed dolefully. He hadn't intended to do anything of the kind. He'd been afraid to press his luck that far. But he didn't really have anything to lose by brazening it out at this point.

She gave a sleepy yawn and stretched against him like a cat.

"No."

Jay's heart plummeted to somewhere in the vicinity of his toes. It would have fallen further if it could have.

Then she sent it soaring with her next words.

"I think it's time you made an honest woman of me."

For several heartbeats, his world hung suspended in space and time. He couldn't breathe.

"I think we should get married," she continued calmly.

Air rushed back into his lungs and he jerked her underneath himself. He pinned her flat with his weight and stared at her.

Jeweled amethyst eyes sparkled back at him.

"Anna, do you mean it?" His voice was taut with tension and his black eyes glittered intensely.

"What, are you waiting for me to get down on my knees?" she scoffed, brows raised in condescension. "Fat chance. If you don't say yes, I'll bash you with my shoes and tie you up with your own tie. Then I'll get Lyle to help me haul you up in front of the judge."

Her threats were music to his ears and returned the rhythm to his heart.

She wanted him. Forever.

She wanted marriage.

She wanted commitment.

And it still wasn't enough, he realized in distant shock. "Anna, I love you," Jay stated roughly. "Don't play with me. I have to know how you feel."

She batted her lashes at him.

"Flat. I feel distinctly flat at the moment."

"You're going to feel more than that in a minute if you don't answer me," he threatened.

"Ha! I knew it all along. I just knew you were into spanking," Anna teasingly accused him, as if her backside wasn't in dire jeopardy of a sincere paddling.

"Answer me," he insisted.

"No. I asked first, you answer me." Then she impudently stuck her tongue out at him, Jay noted, incredulous.

"I must be nuts," he said finally. How could he say no to the one thing he wanted most?

Anna wanted him and she was willing to commit, publicly and legally.

She'd never wanted any other man.

She'd given herself to him completely.

She'd learn to love him, if she didn't yet, Jay vowed fiercely. He'd woo her, romance her and lay a thousand sneaky traps for her heart.

"Yes, Anna, I want to marry you," Jay said seriously.

Her smile widened. "Good. I'm glad that's settled. Good night."

She closed her eyes and feigned sleep.

Jay frowned. "Some genius. A truly smart woman would know when to quit," he warned her. "Stop teasing me. You're baiting the bear."

She raised her head to give him a sweet kiss. "But you're not really a bear, Jay. You're an otter on the inside, remember?"

He gave a fierce growl that would have done credit to a grizzly. "Don't count on it."

She laughed, not in the least concerned.

Until he flipped her over his lap, her bottom in the air.

"No!" She shrieked and struggled to shield herself from his vengeance but she was laughing too hard to be effective. Giving up, she resorted to pleading for mercy. "No, please. Please, Jay."

He shot back, "Please, what? Please don't?"

Anna collapsed in a helpless heap against him, laughing harder than she ever remembered laughing in her life.

Jay let out a disgusted sigh and righted her.

"You should have been born a few hundred years ago," he muttered darkly. "Men back then would have known how to deal with you."

She smiled sweetly back at him. "You'd give me up to another man?"

He gave her a black look that made him appear as devilish and dangerous as he'd first seemed, before he opened his mouth and started to tease and proposition her.

"You know the answer to that, precious. I'd break the arms of any man who laid a hand on you."

That sobered her. "Jay, I have something to tell you."

He swore loudly and inventively. "Now what? Anna, I swear, if you tell me you want some kind of New Age open marriage, I really will spank you until you're black and blue. And don't think I'll let you be on top until it's better, either."

Anna jabbed his ribs with a sharp elbow. "Oh, cut it out, Jay. You'd never do something like that and you know it."

"Don't bet on it."

She sat up and straddled his thighs at that statement. Her long legs hugged his waist and she laid her cheek against his shoulder. A waterfall of flaming curls tumbled over them both, wrapping them in a fiery cloak.

"But I would bet on it, Jay," she said seriously. "You're gentle and kind. You're generous, sensitive, tender and caring. You're strong and loving and giving."

He realized with a start that she was crying. "Anna. Baby, don't cry. Please don't cry," he begged, hugging her closer. "I didn't mean to scare you, angel. Don't cry."

She sniffled loudly and wiped her tears on his bare chest. "I'll cry if I feel like it," she announced. "I have emotions, too, you know. I'm a woman, not some soulless thing."

"I know you are, baby," Jay agreed, rocking her.

"I have feelings, too," she sobbed. "You're not the only one who's in love."

"I know, honey, I—" Jay cut off abruptly as her words sank in. "What?"

She brushed more tears from her cheeks and buried her face in his chest. "I said, I love you."

When he continued to sit, frozen and silent, she jabbed him in the ribs again. "Don't act so surprised. You think scientists can't fall in love?"

He grinned slowly, a wave of happiness rising from his toes to his head. "Oh, sweetheart. You really love me?"

Anna nodded and burrowed deeper into his embrace. Jay automatically tightened his arms, cradling her and soothing her.

"Then why are you crying?"

"Because," she grumbled crossly. "I had plans, too. I was going to romance you and make you swoon. Then I was going to tell you. You messed it all up," she accused.

She didn't seem to notice how ridiculous it sounded.

Jay wasn't about to point it out to her, either.

She'd just handed him all his dreams on a silver platter and a smart man didn't question a gift like that.

"You can start all over. How about that, honey?" he suggested helpfully.

"No. It's too late. You already know now."

Jay hid a smile against her hair. She was something else. As unpredictable, explosive and brilliant as the fireworks she made.

"You could tell me again," he offered.

Anna grew quiet under his soothing hands. He continued to hold her and offer comfort. And wait.

"I love you, Jay. I love you so much. And I didn't even know it," she added, sounding so surprised that he was glad she couldn't see his grin.

If Anna thought he was laughing at her, they'd have to start all over again.

"I'm glad, sweetheart," he answered.

She didn't respond and after a while, Jay realized that she'd fallen asleep in his arms.

Oh, yes, she was really something else.

He lay down with her, taking care not to wake her as he rearranged her against his sprawling length and tucked the quilt around her.

"Sleep well, love," he whispered. She sighed and curled against him as if she responded to him even in sleep.

Anna loved him.

Jay hugged the knowledge to his heart as tightly as he cuddled her length against his own.

Anna wanted to marry him.

They'd have the wedding in his garden, he decided. Spring was in the air, buds were appearing and leaves were opening almost overnight. The garden would be perfect by the end of May and the apple blossoms would be at their peak.

His beautiful Anna would wear a flowing white dress.

He paused in his daydream and frowned. Who would give his Amazon away?

Nobody, he decided firmly. She belonged to herself. She'd come to him on her own and they'd belong to each other forever.

He could almost see it, his breathtaking bride walking toward him, love shining in her amethyst eyes. They'd begin a new life together with the fresh, green spring around them. He could almost smell the apple blossoms and hear the birdsongs. A morning wedding to signify a new chapter in their lives, as full of sunlight and promise as a perfect May.

And they'd go on, together, forever.

"Forever, Anna," he promised again, hugging her closer. "Just wait. It'll be so beautiful."

He slept then, dreaming of their future and his bride growing rounder and softer with new life. His life. Their baby.

"Anna."

Oh, no. Not again. Not already. She hid from the persistent voice and slid deeper into the warmth surrounding her.

"Anna. Sweetheart. My love."

She wanted to groan. She wanted to kick him. Didn't he ever sleep?

Didn't he ever lose interest in sex?

"Oh, go ahead," she moaned, keeping her eyes stubbornly shut. She rolled onto her back and sprawled in what she hoped was an accessible position. "Go ahead, climb on, just don't wake me up," Anna pleaded.

Low laughter greeted what she considered a very generous offer.

"What a proposition. Let me think about it and get back to you," Jay teased.

"Jay, you have a problem and you need help," she ground out through clenched teeth. "I suggest you get some professional counseling about your sleep disorder."

She then promptly rolled into a ball and burrowed back into the covers, only to have them persistently tugged back.

"Come on, honey, it's morning. Wake up."

"It is not, it's the middle of the night and you are a chronic insomniac!" Anna shrieked in helpless fury.

Jay only laughed. "Come on, love." He cuddled her in an attempt to appease her, she supposed. "It really is morning. I let you sleep all night."

She slowly opened one wary eye.

Yes, it was morning all right. Jay wasn't the only source of sunshine in the room. Too much of it streamed brilliantly through the windows.

Anna slipped further under the covers and snuggled against him persuasively. "Jay, let me sleep just a little longer. Please. Please, please, please."

Jay hugged her closer and cupped her belly with one hand. "Don't you want to hear about the wedding plans?"

That cleared away the remnants of sleep in a hurry. There was no telling what he'd come up with while she was sleeping.

"What wedding plans?" Anna opened both eyes wide, forgetting about the sunlight.

That launched him on an unbelievably detailed description of his lunatic plans to hold their wedding outside in his garden. In May.

"Jay, I know I haven't been here all that long but don't you think that's a little risky?" Anna queried.

He gave her a frosty look. "Don't be so negative. It's going to be beautiful. You'll see."

Yes, she would. And if it snowed, she'd laugh until it hurt.

"Are you going to have your friend come and stay for the wedding?" Anna asked, curious.

"Mike?" Jay sounded evasive all of a sudden.

She leaned up on one elbow. "Yes. He's your best friend, isn't he? Don't you want him here?"

"Sure," he said with all the enthusiasm of a man planning a funeral instead of a wedding.

Anna gave him a sharp look. "Don't you want me to meet him?"

Jay sank down on the bed and sighed. "Listen," he began in a low, dispirited voice. "He's my best friend. He can't help how he looks."

Anna frowned. From the sound of it, she thought the poor man must be terribly disfigured in some way. Come to think of it, it was kind of odd that Jay didn't have a picture of his best friend.

"Was he in some kind of accident? I'll be sensitive," Anna promised. "I won't stare."

"Yes, you will," Jay stated mournfully. "You won't be able to help yourself. You'll stare and stare. And drool. He has that effect on women."

She stared at him in disbelief. So it was the opposite problem? And Jay was insecure? Now that was funny. But she hid a smile and said solemnly, "Then I really promise not to stare."

"Sure, you say that now." Jay shot her a wounded look. "I lost every girlfriend I had in college to him. He goes through women the way other guys go through socks. Only faster. We called him the Terminator."

Anna laughed at his dramatics.

"He has this idea about the perfect woman," Jay continued. "He thinks he'll know her right away, so if he doesn't connect on the first date, the poor girl never gets a second chance."

"Well, I think that's nice. He just wants the right person."

Jay quirked a brow at her. "Yeah, and I hope he finds her soon or he'll run out of single women and start looking at other men's wives."

She smiled, amused by his uncharacteristic pessimism.

"Jay." She trailed a finger down his chest to get his attention. "I love you."

He perked up slightly. "Yeah? More than rockets?"

Anna nodded, keeping her face serious with an effort. "Oh, yes. You're much more exciting than explosives. More mysterious than Greek Fire."

A slow smile spread over his face. "Tell me more," Jay invited.

"Well." Anna considered him thoughtfully as her wandering hand moved lower to close over him in a breathtaking caress. "There's also your amazing ability to retain structural integrity under velocity stress."

Jay sighed happily and pulled her underneath him, the better to demonstrate his structural integrity.

"I love it when you talk dirty to me."

The End

THE
☥ ELLORA'S CAVE ☥
LIBRARY

Stay up to date with Ellora's Cave Titles in
Print with our Quarterly Catalog.

To recieve a catalog,
send an email with your name
and mailing address to:

CATALOG@ELLORASCAVE.COM

or send a letter or postcard
with your mailing address to:

Catalog Request
c/o Ellora's Cave Publishing, Inc.
1056 Home Avenue
Akron, Ohio 44310-3502

COMING TO A BOOKSTORE NEAR YOU!

ELLORA'S CAVE

Bestselling Authors Tour

UPDATES AVAILABLE AT

WWW.ELLORASCAVE.COM

ELLORA'S CAVEMEN

LEGENDARY TAILS

Try an e-book for your immediate
reading pleasure or order these titles in print from

WWW.ELLORASCAVE.COM

ELLORA'S CAVE
THE BEST IN TODAY'S ROMANTICA™

MAKE EACH DAY MORE *EXCITING* WITH OUR

ELLORA'S CAVEMEN Calendar

www.EllorasCave.com

erridwen, the Celtic Goddess of wisdom, was the muse who brought inspiration to storytellers and those in the creative arts. Cerridwen Press encompasses the best and most innovative stories in all genres of today's fiction. Visit our site and discover the newest titles by talented authors who still get inspired - much like the ancient storytellers did, once upon a time.

Cerridwen Press

www.cerridwenpress.com

Why an electronic book?

We live in the Information Age—an exciting time in the history of human civilization in which technology rules supreme and continues to progress in leaps and bounds every minute of every hour of every day. For a multitude of reasons, more and more avid literary fans are opting to purchase e-books instead of paperbacks. The question to those not yet initiated to the world of electronic reading is simply: *why?*

1. *Price.* An electronic title at Ellora's Cave Publishing and Cerridwen Press runs anywhere from 40-75% less than the cover price of the <u>exact same title</u> in paperback format. Why? Cold mathematics. It is less expensive to publish an e-book than it is to publish a paperback, so the savings are passed along to the consumer.

2. *Space.* Running out of room to house your paperback books? That is one worry you will never have with electronic novels. For a low one-time cost, you can purchase a handheld computer designed specifically for e-reading purposes. Many e-readers are larger than the average handheld, giving you plenty of screen room. Better yet, hundreds of titles can be stored within your new library—a single microchip. (Please note that Ellora's Cave and Cerridwen Press does not endorse any specific brands. You can check our website at www.ellorascave.com or

www.cerridwenpress.com for customer recommendations we make available to new consumers.)

3. *Mobility.* Because your new library now consists of only a microchip, your entire cache of books can be taken with you wherever you go.

4. *Personal preferences are accounted for.* Are the words you are currently reading too small? Too large? Too...**ANNOYING**? Paperback books cannot be modified according to personal preferences, but e-books can.

5. *Instant gratification.* Is it the middle of the night and all the bookstores are closed? Are you tired of waiting days—sometimes weeks—for online and offline bookstores to ship the novels you bought? Ellora's Cave Publishing sells instantaneous downloads 24 hours a day, 7 days a week, 365 days a year. Our e-book delivery system is 100% automated, meaning your order is filled as soon as you pay for it.

Those are a few of the top reasons why electronic novels are displacing paperbacks for many an avid reader. As always, Ellora's Cave and Cerridwen Press welcomes your questions and comments. We invite you to email us at service@ellorascave.com, service@cerridwenpress.com or write to us directly at: 1056 Home Ave. Akron OH 44310-3502.

Discover for yourself why readers can't get enough of the multiple award-winning publisher Ellora's Cave. Whether you prefer e-books or paperbacks, be sure to visit EC on the web at www.ellorascave.com for an erotic reading experience that will leave you breathless.

www.ellorascave.com